# ONE BREATH AFTER ANOTHER

*THE AFTER ANOTHER TRILOGY, BOOK 2*

BETHANY-KRIS

Published by Bethany-Kris

www.bethanykris.com

ISBN 13: 978-1-989658-32-1

Editor: Elizabeth Peters

Cover Design © London Miller

National Sexual Assault Hotline: 800.656.HOPE (4673)
Chat Online: online.rainn.org

# CONTENTS


PROLOGUE........1
1........3
2........13
3........26
4........32
5........41
6........49
INTERLUDE: 1........57
7........60
8........64
9........69
10........75
11........82
12........88
13........94
INTERLUDE: 2........100
14........103
15........112
16........120
17........131
18........138
19........143
CODA........147
ABOUT THE AUTHOR........149
OTHER BOOKS........150

# PROLOGUE.

*Penny*

*Present Day …*

THERE was something to be said for returning to a place where it all began … at least, in Penny's world. One might think the start of her life—good or bad—had been at the New Jersey home tucked deep within a gated community where her parents kept a permanent residence until her father found himself locked behind bars for his misdeeds.

All the horrors of the three-level Victorian home were hidden by tall, green hedges and a manicured lawn. The luxury vehicles that used to sit in the driveway, and the picture-perfect image her parents presented to the world kept suspicion at bay from anyone who dared to look beyond the pretty surface to find the cracked layers underneath.

And even so, that had been where her life began.

Right?

*Wrong.*

Penny's life started somewhere else. Or what she considered to be the start of it, anyway. Was life really a life worth living if someone didn't know what love was, or how to love? Was life at all important when one wasn't really *living* it, only existing?

That came later for her.

Learning how to live, that was.

It was also every reason why instead of returning to New Jersey … she found herself back in New York. Or specifically, walking the bumpy, dirt path—one of many—that connected the forested area behind Rosalynn and Nazio Donati's home and their rear property.

Was it too close for comfort?

Yes.

Was she being foolish?

Absolutely.

It was … more days than she cared to count since she went AWOL from The League. She didn't doubt for a second that her former handlers already had a small army looking for her. She was a situation they needed to get under control, and they would certainly try to do just that by whatever means necessary.

It also changed nothing.

Penny was done following orders that would not serve her best interests, or the interests of the people who she had done this for in the first place. She wasn't going to make it easy on The League—or anyone else that dared to get in her way—while she finished her business with Allegra Dunsworth.

She shouldn't have come back to Naz and Roz when they would undoubtedly be the first place The League came to look for Penny. Very few others knew her past like her handlers did, though, so she was willing to take the risk. It wasn't like she planned to stay for long.

And yet, despite it all, Penny couldn't help but come back one more time before everything changed again. Before *she* changed everything.

She didn't plan to show herself or even walk up and knock on the backdoor. Her adoptive family would never even know she had been there after she left. They deserved better than a random appearance and another disappearance. She threw their world into upheaval once just by being there and then again when she left without an explanation. There was no good reason to do it to them again. Even she knew that.

No, she just wanted to … see them.

Or their home, rather.

Remind herself why she was here in the first place and what brought her to the point that she was willing to … give it all up.

Her protection from being who she was. The family she desperately missed. A career that had allowed her both healing and retribution for the wrongs done to her. The chance to start over, or to *be* someone else, even.

To learn what came *after* …

All of it and more.

Penny was giving it up—or any chance of it by doing what she had done, really.

Still, as she lingered at the edge of the forest, ten feet beyond where the treeline ended on Naz and Roz's property, she couldn't help but think it was still worth it. For them, and their life, even if it was one without her.

And for her, too.

For her peace of mind. Something she never had—not while her mother still walked and breathed.

Soon, Allegra wouldn't.

Penny needed to start over first. Go back to the beginning and *remember.* To know that for a time, before all of this happened, she was happy. Or … she was starting to learn how to be happy in her own way. Until her mother ruined that, too.

Some things never changed …

Lost in her thoughts and still staring at the only home she had ever known, Penny was too distracted to hear the crack of twigs from her left. That was, until a little voice said, "Hey, Penny."

# 1.

*Luca*

*Six and a half years earlier …*

SOMETIMES, the present was the last place Luca wanted to be, but especially when nothing he did seemed to please anyone around him. That was never more obvious than when he sat at his family's dinner table. Even a simple question wasn't just a question for him to answer regardless of which parent asked it of him.

It was always an opening for a discussion. One of *many*, unfortunately. Discussions that made it very clear he wasn't doing what someone thought he should be, but certainly when it came to his life choices.

"How were your classes this week?" his mother asked.

Luca stabbed the waffle on his plate with a fork, hoping that if he shoved the bite into his mouth and chewed for long enough, Katya would forget she even asked in the first place. *Highly unlikely.*

"All right," he muttered around chews when she continued staring at him from her spot at the end of the table. "Missed a lecture and my morning classes but—"

"Education is important, Luca."

*Yeah, here we go*, he thought.

"And you *did* want to go to college," Katya added after a moment. "Why waste time and resources if you're unwilling to commit to your choice?"

"I'm not wasting anything, Ma."

"Don't talk with your mouth full."

*Christ.*

Maybe he had looked at this all wrong. Instead of using bites of food to deflect his mother's questions about his failing attempt at law school—every good criminal family needed a defense lawyer, right?—she was using his full mouth as a chance to get her opinion in when he couldn't talk back.

Sneaky.

But smart.

Also, not surprising.

Wives of made men learned different ways over the years about just how they could get their voices heard when it wasn't meant to be in the discussion in the first place. His mother might have been given a bit more freedom in her place as his father's wife—not *all* made men cared to have compliant, silent, pretty dolls for wives, after all—but she also knew where the lines were drawn when it came to the family business.

While his father watched them from his chair at the head of the table, he knew his mother was toeing the line by even bringing up the fact that his higher education was currently taking a hit as he stepped more and more into Zeke's business.

The family business.

The *mafia.*

"I just think—"

"Katya," his father spoke up, drawing all attention to Zeke when he picked up his coffee mug from the table. "Would you mind pouring me another cup? This one is cold."

Luca's mother sighed.

His father would never outright tell her to stop pushing the topic. Zeke wouldn't shut his wife up just because she asked things that he didn't like. He would, however, divert her on to something else which was a clear but silent *that's quite enough, darling.*

The chair legs squeaked against the tiled floor of the dining room as Katya stood from the table with pursed lips. A good sign of her displeasure, not that she would voice it with Luca there. He couldn't remember—in all of his twenty-four, almost twenty-five years—a time when his parents fought in front of him or his younger sister, Roz. Hell, his mother never even raised her voice despite the little shit he had been as a kid.

Zeke, on the other hand …

He didn't mind being loud.

"*Grazie*," Zeke thanked his wife when she took the cup from his hand as she passed.

"You're welcome."

"Am I?" his father asked under his breath after his wife had left the dining room entirely. "That'll be a fun chat later, I'm sure."

Zeke went back to looking over the newspaper beside his breakfast plate like the entire thing hadn't happened in the first place. Luca wasn't quite as willing to pretend.

"You don't have to do that," he told his father. "I can handle Ma's questions. She's just … worried."

"Because you're doing what you should be doing?"

"Because she's not sure it's what I *want* to do."

The mafia wasn't for the faint of heart, but especially not a man who was just beginning to dabble in the business. He was at the beck and call of any man in the Donati crime family who needed or wanted him for whatever they thought would serve their purposes. He barely had time to sleep and feed himself lately, let alone get any of the many papers done for college that had been due … a long time ago.

He *should* just quit.

He rarely made it to class anymore. His grades were inconsequential because he wasn't even doing the work to *get* a fucking grade. Katya had been right in stating he was wasting time and resources, but wrong that she assumed they were his to do so.

Someone else could take his spot at college. The money his parents paid for him to attend was someone else's *dream.* He was very aware of his privilege and the fact he abused it. Luca wasn't that much of an asshole that he didn't care.

It wasn't that at all.

He just …

"Roz is a fucking pianist prodigy," he muttered, referring to his little sister—by only a year—that would soon be returning from her stay in Australia where she had played for a massive company for several years. "My best friend is a literal genius."

Naz, that was.

Who also dated his sister.

Luca shrugged, pushing the food around on his plate because now it looked a little less appealing than before if only because he wasn't in the mood to eat anymore. A sense of unworthiness could do that to a person. He hated feeling like he wasn't up to par with the people around him. Not that anyone ever voiced as much.

His parents didn't compare him to his genius friend or musically inclined sister. Luca did that all on his own because he heard the things that *were* said and made of them what he wanted or needed to at any given time.

Zeke eyed him over the edge of the newspaper, considering that before he replied, "And you're … what?"

"Exactly. What am I, Papa?"

"What you should be, Luca."

Was he?

"I wanted to be a defense lawyer," he said.

Zeke sucked air through his teeth, saying, "I think you're doing right by focusing on the family business. You balanced both for a while, but it's hard to deny that one is now starting to suffer. Surprise, you need to make a hard choice. Comes with adulthood, son. We all reach those points eventually. You've hit yours."

"And if I didn't want college to suffer—"

"Luca."

Right.

*There it is …*

That tone of his father's—one he knew all too well. His mother didn't want him to quit college, and his father didn't care what Luca did as long as he worked to be a made man. Just like Zeke—or any other man in his life that really mattered.

It was *expected*.

Luca used to think he could do both. He even dared people to prove him differently, and they hadn't been able to for a time.

The pressure came from all sides.

Constantly.

He was really getting tired of trying to please everyone instead of just doing what *he* wanted. The problem was, he hadn't found what he wanted to do yet. Which was exactly why he was trying to do everything.

*And failing*.

"I'll tell your mother to lay off a bit on the college thing," Zeke told him.

Luca only thought, *but what about you*? What about the fact that his father made it clear he believed his only son should have his life all figured out by now and nothing else would do?

Not that he said it out loud.

It wouldn't matter.

The beep of his phone distracted Luca momentarily. Just long enough for him to pull the device from the pocket of his jeans and check the message that lit up the screen.

*Be at the club in Brooklyn in two hours. I've got a problem*, it read.

What was more surprising was the fact that it came from Naz who was supposed to be overseas visiting with Roz before accompanying her home. She was finally coming back from Australia. *For good*.

But if Naz was already back and hadn't even told Luca as much, then—

"Where are you going?" Katya asked, returning from the kitchen with a steaming mug of coffee in hand for her husband only to find Luca standing from the table. "You didn't even finish breakfast. This is the only time all week I've even been able to see you, Luca."

"Sorry, Ma," he muttered, giving his father a pleading look to excuse him while he pulled his leather jacket from the back of the chair. "An emergency came up with Naz. I gotta go."

"But—"

"Let him go, Katya," Zeke said. "Family business first."

His mother sighed.

*Loudly*.

She at least gave him a smile when he dropped a kiss to her cheek on the way by. Not that it reached her eyes or felt particularly true.

He also didn't mind running out early despite the tinge of guilt that pulled at his gut. He didn't want to keep disappointing his mother—or even his father.

But shit …

Whatever got him out of that house.

• • •

Naz said two hours.

Luca made it forty-five minutes early because he got lucky and traffic wasn't completely fucking horrible on the way over.

His good fortune meant he wasn't surprised that he arrived before Naz at the Brooklyn club affectionally known around the family as *Dizzy's* because of the manager. A female that barely touched five feet in height but was known for her ability to gut a grown man without a blink. Despite being told by *many* men in *la famiglia* that Nazio should hire someone more appropriate—like a guy—to run the place for him while he only used the club mainly to work *out of* for more illegal business, his best friend refused. Deserie—or Dizzy, to the people who mattered—knew how to do her job and that's what mattered the most.

It spoke to the changes in Cosa Nostra's culture over the years, even since his own father's days. Especially when those first few men who voiced their displeasure at a woman so close to *the* business were also quick to accept a younger man's perspective on how certain aspects of said business should be done.

Because Naz wasn't wrong.

It probably helped too that the boss of the family enjoyed challenging the opinions and views of those around him simply because he could. Oh, and because the boss was Naz's own father. If anything, it afforded Luca's friend a stronger position in the decisions he made regarding the mafia.

Luca wished he could say the same. Having a father that held one of the highest seats in the Donati crime family only aided in the expectations that followed him around nonstop. While his friend managed to handle that same pressure with a grace that said Naz was meant to be the son of a boss, he was left feeling like he wasn't good enough.

Which was some kind of shit, that.

No one ever said as much.

Luca was just … *fucked* that way, maybe. In his head or because he read too much into the way his parents voiced their love *and* worries. Who knew?

Not him.

"You're looking … in a mood," came a dark, familiar voice from Luca's left as he stepped beyond the entrance of the club.

He did his best not to show his surprise at hearing Naz's father greet him. He found Cross sitting in the first booth in a line of many, a lit cigar dancing between his lips as he muttered to the man sitting across from him to say, "Give me fifteen, Marty, yeah?"

"Sure, boss."

The man stood from the booth and didn't look back at the stacks of cash he left behind on the table.

Cross offered Luca a smile as he pulled the cigar from his mouth and said, "What—cat got your tongue?"

"Nah, I just—"

"Lighten up, Luca. I was kidding. Sit for a minute. Indulge my arrogant company, hmm?"

Cross waved at the seat across from his, but Luca took in the bar around them, still wondering why the Donati crime boss was there in the first place. He did business in a lot of places—not *here.* The place didn't look the same in the daylight. One could actually see how large the stained, glossy wood floor was and the sixty feet it spanned from one side to the wall-to-wall bar on the other side.

It wasn't the *best* club. A bit shoddy in appearance, it certainly wasn't the usual, upscale place where one would find made men doing business.

They still liked it.

"Well, *sit,*" Cross told him, sharper the second time with a pointed look at the booth and then Luca, directly.

He did.

Even though he grew up calling this man his uncle—and Cross was also his godfather—the older Luca became, the better he understood that Cross was also *more.* And he demanded respect because of it, too. His relationship changed with the man accordingly. He was still the guy who took Luca and Naz sledding on winter break when they were kids.

But he was also the same man that Luca watched beat an enforcer to death with his fists because he slighted Cross's wife, Catherine, and her family—another major crime family based in New York.

Luca never forgot it, either.

Cross grabbed a stack of the money, licking his thumb before he started swiping through the bills, asking Luca at the same time, "You here for Naz?"

"Yeah. How'd you know?"

A shrug answered him, along with Cross's chuckled, "Why do you think I'm here? My son took off like a bat out of hell overseas, and then suddenly he's showing back up much the same way he left. I would like a reason why, but also … his mother is worried."

Luca fought a smile. "Yeah, they do that. Mothers, I mean."

"Hmm. And don't think I forgot about that mood, either."

"What?"

Cross grinned. "You know *what.*"

He did.

Luca had also hoped the man would drop it. He couldn't be so lucky. "Nothing, really. Just shit in my head that shouldn't be there in the first place. Since when do you do business in Dizzy's, anyway?"

"Since I felt like picking up someone's tab today while I was here and had the time," Cross replied. "And whenever else I feel like it. We're busy men, Luca, I don't expect you to know what a boss does with his days or time."

He heard the warning.

An unspoken: *Don't question me.*

It wasn't malicious, he knew. Just … a part of who they were. Or rather, who *Cross* was. The boss answered nothing and no one.

"Sorry," he was quick to mutter at Cross's stare. "Even Dad still has to tell me to watch my mouth every once and a while."

"That's what fathers are for. Well, *that* and driving their sons up the wall like their fathers used to do to them. Tradition, or some shit. We pass all of that on to our boys hoping they push the lines even more than we did when we had the chance with our own way back. Not that we would ever tell you that, mind."

Luca's brow dipped. "Were you talking to my father?"

"What?"

He shook his head, replying, "Never mind."

"I don't need to speak with Zeke about you to see when you're struggling, Luca," Cross murmured, drawing his gaze back to the man watching him from the other side of the booth. "I know things are different between us from when you were a boy, but there is still a part of me that *sees* and remembers that boy very well."

*Right.*

Of course, his godfather would see shit was up.

"I *am* dealing with it," he told Cross.

"And what is it, exactly?"

"I don't really know."

It was the truth.

Because it was everything.

And nothing at all.

"You know," Cross said, slapping the stack of now-counted bills to the table and plucking up another, "it *is* okay to not know things, or even, need time to figure it out. Or if you're anything like I was as a young man on the cusp of making big decisions in my adulthood … take a hatchet in swinging and build your own fucking path. No one option is right for every person."

Luca laughed hard, not expecting *that*. "I'll keep it in mind. Do you know what the emergency is? Naz, I mean. Because there's no way he took off and came back like he did without—"

"Something being wrong," Cross finished for him. "You're right. And yes, I know. He at least had *enough* sense to fill me in."

But clearly, the man wasn't going to tell Luca about what.

*Well …*

He could wait.

• • •

Naz showed up an hour late.

Luca didn't mind. He waited for his friend even after Cross said he had to leave—another commitment he couldn't put off, apparently.

"Where's my dad?" Naz asked. The first question out of his mouth when he stepped inside the club. "I thought he was going to stick around to talk."

"Business never stops."

Well, that was what Cross told Luca. He was just repeating the sentiment.

"And he said you could catch him up," Luca added. "What's up?"

Naz joined Luca in the booth with a heavy sigh. He scrubbed his palms over his face, and rolled his shoulders as he settled in. It was probably the most disheveled his friend had ever looked—his clothes were pristine, of course, but Luca found the truth in Naz's face. Dark circles under his eyes and stress lines deep between his eyes like he'd been scowling for days.

"Have you even slept?"

"Not in three days," Naz admitted. "It's been …"

"Roz is okay, right?" Luca asked.

He figured she was okay if only because his friend wouldn't hide that from Rosalynn's family. If something was wrong with his sister, he would have known about it when Nazio first took off overseas without warning.

"She's … great," Naz settled on saying. "We both are. It's not her."

"Then, what's going on?"

Naz glanced away, eyeing the booth across from theirs while he rubbed his hands together and shook his head. "A girl. Penny."

"Who?"

"*Penny*," Naz said again. "A pianist prodigy Kyle wanted Roz to meet on her way home. He intended for her to maybe mentor the girl or something but, shit didn't go down that way."

"Fucking Kyle."

His sister's mentor was something else sometimes. The man had been beneficial for Roz's career, but he was also one of those most annoying human beings on the earth. His *music over everything* philosophy didn't exactly jam with their family values, either.

"Kyle's not important," Naz muttered, waving a hand. "The girl is."

"Right. Penny, you said?"

"Penny Dunsworth."

Why did that name sound familiar? It took him a minute to connect it to someone he knew—or rather, a man he knew *of*.

"Like the New Jersey family—*that* Dunsworth? Guy's a multi-billionaire from overseas investments, right?"

"Also a fucking pedophile, apparently."

Luca stiffened in the booth. "What?"

"She's sixteen, almost seventeen," Naz explained. "And in a *bad* way with an equally bad history, man. She tried to hang herself while Roz was there with Kyle. That kind of bad, Luca. Anyway, after that happened is when I showed up. They committed her, but Roz got it in her head how she wanted to help."

That sounded like Roz.

But … "Help, how?"

Naz chuckled sadly. "I guess they got her talking in the institution when the topic came up about sending her home to Jersey. She's got proof of what her father's been doing to her for years … there was no way Roz was going to let her go back there. They're just waiting for the American officials to take over the investigation at this point because … well, it's a whole mess."

*Shit.*

As sick as he felt, Luca knew what his friend was trying to say without just saying it outright. "Roz wants you guys to bring her home."

"Yeah."

"And you're okay with that?"

Naz shrugged helplessly. "I don't know how to tell her it's a bad idea … I'm also not sure that it is. The girl needs help. *Real* help and not just for the shit that's happened to her in private but also *her*. She needs people to help her."

"You wanna be those people?"

"Roz does," Naz murmured. "I want what Roz wants."

Just like that.

*Simple.*

Luca respected it, even. It was why he never had an issue with his best friend dating his sister because the guy was gold. *Good.* Naz treated Roz like a fucking queen, and everybody knew it. What more could they want?

Hell, this situation would probably uproot his friend's entire life, but Naz just looked … ready for it. Ready to do whatever Roz wanted.

"How can I help?" Luca asked.

It only seemed right.

Naz grinned. "With the girl? Not much. She's like a baby deer—scared of *everything*. And mean sometimes, or that's what Roz says. But you can help me."

"Anything, man."

"Yeah, I know. That's why you're here. I'm going to be busy for a while to make this work and do everything to get it moving forward for Roz, so we can get Penny home and settled in with us. You could handle some things for me with *la famiglia*, right? Keep an eye on my guys and keep up with whatever my father has going on so nothing gets behind. Shit like that."

"I got that, no worries," Luca replied.

Naz sat a little straighter in the booth, his gaze less worried than before. "I figured."

"Some people might not like it, though. Some made men from the family, I mean, but—"

"Fuck them," Naz interrupted, his hand cutting between them to end the subject right then and there. "It's been you and me. Always was, always is. You know?"

Luca nodded. "Yeah, I know."

Some things never changed.

He was okay with that.

# 2.

## *Penny*

THE reflection in the windowpane of Penny's therapist's office in uptown Manhattan was far more interesting than the conversation she was trying to *not* engage. Not that her efforts to ignore the doctor's questions did her any good.

"You've been living with Rosalynn Puzza and Nazio Donati for almost two months now, right?" her doctor asked. "How's that going?"

"Fine."

"And?"

"Nothing."

"Nothing?" the therapist questioned, raising a brow behind Penny.

She could see that in the reflection of the glass, too. As clear as she could see her own, ghostly pale, heart-shaped face. The white-blonde hair that she hadn't washed in more days than she cared to remember curtained her face more than it framed it. She didn't mind. It was easier not to be seen.

Penny didn't want to be looked at. Not by anyone. If only everyone else felt the same way as her. Things would be far easier.

"Your life has been significantly changed in just two months," the therapist said. "You went from living overseas and attending a prestigious private school for the musically inclined to returning back to the states with new guardians. All during handling the police's investigation of your father. It isn't surprising if things are a little … overwhelming for you, Penny."

"And it's fine."

*Usually*, but she didn't add that out loud. It would only encourage the therapist to ask more or probe into the topic, and Penny didn't want to talk in the first place. She was only here doing this because it was a demand made by the social worker that regularly showed up to check in on her and her new guardians.

Roz handled the bitch with grace.

Penny couldn't say the same.

"How about the pregnancy? I understand you have no siblings, so Rosalynn—"

"I call her Roz. It's what she likes."

And since Penny liked Roz, she tried to do what the woman wanted. Like calling her by the name she preferred. It was a simple thing, sure, but if it was anyone else and she *didn't* like them … well, their life would be a far more miserable place.

"Roz, then," the therapist was quick to say behind her, the scratching against paper telling Penny that the woman was writing on her notepad. "How do you feel about Roz's pregnancy? Are you excited for the baby?"

She only shrugged.

"Miss Dunsworth, I don't know what shrugs mean."

Oh, *yay*.

She got the last name.

That usually meant the therapist was starting to catch on that Penny was going to spend their entire hour—one of three every week until the doctor and social worker believed she wasn't a danger to herself anymore—deflecting everything she asked.

"You know," the woman said, not unkindly, "the longer you drag on actually talking to me about certain things, the more time you'll spend with me, Penny."

Well …

She had a point.

Not one Penny particularly liked. Then again, what did she like?

"I don't know how I feel about the pregnancy," Penny said, not bothering to respond to the obvious. "Roz is happy. She and Naz are planning a bunch of stuff. A move, and other shit. They don't forget about me, though. It's like … not *here*, I guess? I can't feel something for someone that's not here, can I?"

She didn't *know* the unborn baby; didn't even know the gender or a name yet. She did enjoy watching Naz and Roz together, but especially when they didn't know she was watching, because she couldn't remember seeing two people who treated each other with such love and care before. Her mother and father had never been like that … more *transactional*. Everything was an equal give and take or even a negotiation. All business.

She hadn't realized relationships weren't really like that, but she wasn't surprised to learn something else about her parents' marriage had been manufactured.

"Your father isn't here. Do you extend the same lack of emotion to the man who raped and sold your body because he isn't present, either?"

*Fuck*.

*Nice segue*, Penny thought. The therapist wasn't getting smarter about how she did that. The entire reason she was sitting in this office and the one thing she didn't want to talk about was the sexual abuse she suffered through with her father.

Hadn't she talked enough?

She was silent for years.

Then, all it took was the mental ward overseas suggesting that she would be transferred back to the care of her mother and father for the floodgates to open. No way in hell was she going back to *them*. She had finally been free, for all purposes. Her parents were satisfied to send her brand of trouble all the way across the world, far away from them.

She liked that fine, too.

Except once she started talking about the things her father had done to her from the time she was two … well, it didn't stop. A doctor turned into another doctor that wanted to take notes. And then a bobby arrived because the doctors had to report it. One officer turned into two, and then the Americans got involved because the majority of abuse took place in Jersey.

She thought one person would be enough, but no. Penny couldn't be so lucky. Now there were fifty hours or more of videotapes with recordings of her speaking in detail about the abuse she suffered for years. Videotapes that they planned to show at her father's trail—*if* she wasn't called to testify herself.

*Christ.*

She talked enough.

Penny didn't want to keep doing it.

"Penny?" the therapist asked softly. "You're very tense over there. Can you let go of your hand for me? I can see the way you're digging your fingernails into the side of your palm. Take a second if you need it."

She needed far more than a second.

A million minutes.

A new memory.

A whole new *life*.

Except that wouldn't happen.

She was who she was.

Fucked up.

Broken inside and out.

*Tired of all of it.*

Eventually, Penny did let go of her hand, ignoring the three, deep red crescent marks she had damn near cut through the skin that were left behind. Thankfully, the therapist didn't continue pressing the topic of Preston Dunsworth. Instead, she moved onto something else that was just about as bad on Penny's *fuck no* radar.

"How do you feel about your mother—Allegra—not attempting to gain custody of you back from your current guardians? I hear you got the news about that development recently, right?"

God.

The woman was a dog digging for a bone. And any bone would do even if it was one she bit out of Penny's body to gnaw on. Because that's exactly how this felt. Yet another reason why she hated therapy with Dr. Tangler. The only reason why she continued returning was the fact that she didn't hate the doctor personally.

Only what she was trying to do—*fix Penny*.

She couldn't be fixed.

"Penny, how do you feel—"

"I *don't*," she snapped.

"Don't feel, you mean?"

"Not for her."

She wouldn't even say her mother's name. *Couldn't*. The pressure in her chest became painful along with the swell of memories that were now ever constant and always on replay in the back of her mind. All these people wanted her to do was remember.

Penny needed to *forget*.

"She's your mother. You're her only child. And you're not at all affected that she's effectively orphaned you to the state?" the woman asked.

"No."

And if Penny were considered mentally stable enough for a proper emancipation, then she would have tried for that, too. That was that. What else needed said?

Penny continued staring at the reflection in the glass, comforted more by the sight of her wide, haunted blue eyes than anything else. *You look like an angel*, her father would tell her. *People pay for the way you look, Penny*. She didn't see that at all, only pain.

At least, her stare didn't lie. Everything anyone needed to know was always staring back at them. She was happy, at least, that the last bit of yellowish bruising on her neck had finally disappeared over the last week. It had been the only reminder of her last suicide attempt.

One of many.

This time would have worked if not for Roz … and Kyle, too, a mentor who had been trying to help Penny overseas. He was long gone, though, back to wherever he spent his days. And she was left with Roz and Naz while the bruises faded from the rope she had tied perfectly.

Penny didn't know whether she was happy or not that they saved her. Everybody says a person only wants to die until they *are* dying, but she didn't remember it that way.

That was part of her depression, she knew. The disconnect. Her lack of desire to talk or even be present. How she would much rather hide beneath blankets or in clothes that drowned her body.

Not soon enough for her liking, the second hand of the clock finally ticked down the last minute of her required therapy session. Another form would be filled out and sent to the social worker to say Penny and her guardians were doing all the work demanded of them to ensure her mental health and well-being.

But as she stood to leave, Dr. Tangler asked, "One to ten this week?"

She didn't need to clarify what she meant. Penny understood.

"Eight."

"That's high on the scale."

"Not the nine it was last week," Penny returned.

"Do you have an active plan?"

"No."

Not one for suicide, anyway.

"Self-harm?" the therapist asked.

It took every ounce of self-control Penny had not to rub at the black, long-sleeve sweater covering her arms. Even the denim of her skinny jeans itched overtop the scars she hid with clothing. The mere mention of her habit to cut was enough to make her *want* to do it. Numbness would follow—it was all she really wanted.

"Not lately," she said honestly.

Penny couldn't say how long it would last.

The therapist didn't ask.

"I'll see you next week," the woman said as Penny left the room.

*Maybe*, she replied silently. She didn't make promises and while she might not be actively planning another suicide attempt, she also didn't plan for anything else, either. Wishful thinking, perhaps. Or it could just be her depression talking again.

That bitch never left.

And neither did—

"How did it go?" Roz asked the second Penny emerged from the office's back hallway. She stood from the waiting room's chair, offering one of her smiles. A warm, comforting sight. Like everything else about Rosalynn Puzza. She just … *drew* people in—made them feel safe. Including Penny, but it was hard to trust that. "Okay, I hope."

Penny shrugged. "Like it usually does."

"I know you don't like coming here but—"

"Required by the state and child services," she interjected, parroting the same shit everybody told her. "I know, Roz."

Plus, it kept her accountable.

Not that Penny would admit it. Then, people might think it was *helping*. Nothing helped.

Roz joined Penny's side as they left the office, stepping out into a busy Manhattan sidewalk. Life bustled all around them, but she felt distanced from it all. Another day alive.

"I know things are going to be busy for the next month while we move into the new house," Roz said, "but your seventeenth birthday is less than a week away."

"And?"

A car pulled up for them.

She didn't ask why Roz had drivers. Or why there were men with guns that kept an eye on the house. Never mind the fact that the last names of her guardians seemed to draw a sense of respect and caution everywhere they went.

"I thought maybe you might want to do something for it," Roz explained.

"Not really."

"Not even dinner?"

Penny sighed. "A day off therapy."

Roz laughed lightly. "Sorry, one thing I can't do."

*Right.*

But her guardians tried to do everything else and that's what counted. After years of people only hurting Penny, she finally had someone—two people, really—who seemed to actually care. She wasn't used to that.

"I think I just want to sleep," Penny said.

"Okay. But if you need anything, even while we're busy moving, just tell me. We'll make it happen, Penny."

Yeah.

She knew.

They just couldn't give her what she needed the most: everything to be *gone.*

• • •

The thing about depression? That shit was a cloud. Heavy, opaque, and *constant.* It followed Penny around, through days that turned into weeks, and melted into months. Time became irrelevant when she was fighting just to make it from one hour to the next.

Before she realized it, two months had passed her by. Two months on top of the two she had already been living in New York with her new guardians. She only came to that understanding because of the DA currently talking at the kitchen table of Roz and Naz's new house.

"We were happy to be able to get this done and settled in such a short time—four months for a case like this is unheard of—so we were happy to agree to the deal with Preston Dunsworth considering the trail would have dragged on for possibly … years."

"Wait," Penny muttered, stopping the DA from saying anything more about this deal they had settled out with her monster of a father and his horrible fucking lawyers. "Go back—so what you're saying is that he'll plead guilty to eighty-five counts of child pornography, right?"

"Yes," the man across the table said.

Underneath, where no one could see, Roz's hand squeezed tightly around Penny's. An ache had settled deep in her heart. Despite the fact she actually hadn't needed to see or speak to her father since this whole thing started …

every time she had to talk about him, or he was brought into a conversation, she felt ill.

She didn't want to think about him anymore. He didn't deserve a space in her mind.

So, why was he still there?

Penny couldn't cut him out.

She *tried*.

"The deal says each count will have time served consecutively, and not together," the DA said, like Penny was a fucking idiot and needed it explained to her again. She heard it just fine the first fucking time. "With the maximum penalty for each charge, that could add up to over—"

"Just shut up," Penny said.

The man gave her a look. "Excuse me?"

"Penny," Roz said quietly beside her. "It's okay … try to say what you're feeling, and not just try to hurt someone else because we're hurting, right?"

God.

Why did Roz have to be like … that?

All the time, too.

"I think," came the dark voice of Naz behind Penny where he leaned against the wall of the kitchen in their new—because a baby needed lots of space, apparently—home, "what Penny is not quite saying but wants to, is that it's just the child porn charges, correct?"

"Yes, those are charges that will be impossible for them to win against."

"And nothing for her."

The man across the table stiffened. "Well—"

Naz didn't allow the man to continue on with whatever in the fuck he planned to say before he added, "So, perhaps you could forgive Penny that you made a deal with the man who raped her, and sold her body for years, wherein he will plead guilty to everything but what he did to her. Because you see, the only reason why you were able to get the child porn and charge him for that was because she came forward … she talked, again and again and again. You put her on tape, you made her relive trauma to stranger after stranger. You put her in front of therapist after therapist to see if she was lying. You promised justice would be served for her."

"Sir—"

"And in fact," Naz continued, "what you did was use her to get what you could from him, and instead of getting her abuser on the stand to admit to what he did to her, she instead gets to feel like everything she did was not actually for her own benefit. So yeah, I think you could empathize with why she needs you to explain again the choice you made. And without the attitude the second time around—go ahead, try it, Mr. Mahoney."

The DA swallowed hard and stared at the wood grain on the dining room table they currently sat at. Roz squeezed Penny's hand again, and she was eternally grateful for the support that she found in this house. It was strange to her in the way that those weren't at all the things she had been expecting when she came to live here with Naz and Roz.

Penny had become so used to being alone—to feeling numb to all and anything in her life—that now, it felt like she experienced too much when it came to her emotions, and she didn't know the first damn thing to do with them.

She was getting better, though.

One step at a time.

It was terrifying.

"Trial would be long," the DA murmured, "and drawn out. Media would be all over it—constantly. Penny would likely have to testify. No doubt in front of a packed courtroom, we'd be lucky if we were able to get a media ban approved by the judge, and certainly in full view of her father where he could stare at her while she retold detail after detail of his abuse. Which, again no doubt, would be for his pleasure, and certainly not for hers. So yes, I understand that on the surface, this deal doesn't exactly seem like it is to Penny's benefit—"

"Not one bit," Penny replied sharply.

"But your other options will be far more traumatic. He will die in prison, and it might not be because he admitted to the things he did to you, but it will be because of the strength and courage you have shown time and time again to make sure he couldn't do this to someone else."

Penny let out a shaky breath.

Why didn't that help?

Wordlessly, Penny stood from the table. Roz looked her way, a silent request for her to stay and finish the conversation. It reflected in the woman's eyes, but Penny couldn't do what she wanted. Right now, she just needed to be alone … or something.

Anything but this.

Roz always told her that was okay, too.

To be alone.

To need time.

It was okay, and she could take it.

As she headed out of the kitchen without as much as a look over her shoulder, Penny heard the DA say, "We don't need her agreement on the deal for it to go through, but I did want to let her know personally."

"Right," Naz snapped back, "because it is never about the victim, only the victory."

"Or do you just have a personal problem with law enforcement, Nazio Donati, because of your own circumstances?"

"Get the fuck out of my house."

Penny heard the front door slam shut minutes later, but she was already at the back of the house, sitting in front of the piano that taunted her on a daily basis. For whatever reason, she hadn't been able to play it since she arrived in New York. It followed them from the penthouse to the large, three-level home in the suburbs.

Roz played.

Naz did, occasionally, even if it wasn't perfect.

Penny, though?

Never.

Until right now. The urge thrummed deep, the notes taking shape in her mind the longer she stared at the glossy black smoothness of the piano legs.

Why now?

Why when she shouldn't care?

Why did it matter now?

*Good girls play for Daddy,* she heard him say in her head. *Oh, you missed a key, what does that mean?* And then, *Smile at the camera when you do that, Penny, they like it.*

"Fuck you, fuck you … *fuck you,*" Penny mumbled, rocking forward on the bench. "Just … fuck you."

She pressed the heels of her palms to her burning eyes as she squeezed them shut, willing his voice out of her head, and for those memories to burn. Maybe that's what she had been looking for here, to take away all of that, but it was never going to go away.

Those memories would never leave.

It would never not *be.*

Her fingers trembled as she placed them to the ivory, the tune that came out of the instrument echoing and haunting through the halls of the quiet house as it matched the sounds she made when she cried.

And *God.*

She cried so hard.

The melody was so unlike what she had been known to play before—much darker, and deafening. A tune that had goosebumps racing over her skin and had her heart thumping hard against her ribcage.

It was pain.

Not pain she caused.

Not pain he made.

It didn't come from a razor against her skin, and it didn't hurt. It wasn't brought on by wrongs done to her, even if memories helped to create the music. It didn't leave scars behind, and it didn't linger long enough to make her wish she wasn't here at all.

It was pain put into music.

And it felt different like that.

Better like that.

For a long time, Penny had pushed music aside because it felt like a punishment. She had been put in front of a piano for her father's desire, not because anyone thought she would be any good at it. Her talents had then been used to please others, before they turned it around on her so that when she misbehaved, they punished her with it, too.

By sending her away with the music.

And she hated them.

Hated it.

But this was none of that.

This was all her.

Why couldn't everything else be like that, too?

• • •

The weeks that followed the DA showing up with news of the plea agreement with Penny's father wasn't … good. Quite the opposite for her. She hadn't known what she expected from finally putting her father in prison, but the emptiness settling deep within the pit of her gut certainly wasn't *it*.

The darkness of the bedroom that belonged to her in the large home stared back at Penny. She couldn't say how many hours she laid there watching the ceiling, but it was a few. A few more than she should. The dark shades she had pulled closed in the morning kept any light from coming in which meant she couldn't even estimate the time by looking at the sky.

What did it matter?

She *wished* she cared.

It was the buzz of her phone that pulled her from the depths of dark, spiraling thoughts that always led her to a dangerous edge whenever she had enough time to indulge. Without even checking the text, she knew it was from Roz.

She was right.

The guilt that spread around her heart—like tentacles squeezing the blood right out of the beating organ—at the sight of the message was impossible to ignore. Penny knew why, too. She hadn't even read the words yet, but she didn't need to when the only thing Roz ever did was make sure her ward was okay.

All the time.

*Whenever.*

Roz cared more about Penny than even her own mother had. She worried about the teenager constantly even though she tried not to voice it too much.

Penny wanted to be good for Roz—desperately wished she could say she was okay and mean it every time her guardian asked—but she still hadn't learned how to do that for herself, yet. How was she supposed to do it for someone else?

The actual text of the message made her feel worse when Roz asked, *How are your classes today?*

Not great.

Because she skipped.

Penny didn't lie in her reply—a simple: *Came back home early*—because it was the only thing her two guardians asked of her. That she always tell them the truth no matter how uncomfortable or painful it might be. At least then, they could help her if needed. They didn't want the truth to punish her for it.

Something else she wasn't used to.

*Okay*, came Roz's next reply. *Not because of someone, right?*

No, just her depression.

Penny only texted back: *No.*

It didn't seem to bother Roz at all because her next reply, a far longer message, dropped the subject altogether. Not that Penny was excited to see the words on the screen, far too bright in the darkness of the room.

*If you're home and have time, then, would you look over the file from the lawyer? He sent it over a week ago, and he really needs you to sign it, Penny. I know you don't care about the trust fund or restitution payment, but he does need to file it for the estate.*

Her first thought was to say hell no. The very idea of taking money from her father and his estate fucked her up more than anything else in her life currently. She had been avoiding that file sitting on the desk in the corner of her bedroom since Naz put it there.

She didn't want shit from Preston. Hadn't her father *given* her enough? Penny thought so.

Still, it had to be done.

Otherwise, the lawyer would continue to pester Naz and Roz, who wouldn't say a thing to Penny about it because they didn't push. But the file would remain on her desk where she had to look at it every day knowing the final payment for her innocence waited for her signature.

More blood money. Cash for her silence. At least this time, Penny was the one being paid.

Right?

*Fuck.*

She hated how morbid her thoughts could be sometimes. Another hell she couldn't escape.

Penny didn't bother to reply to Roz's last message. Instead, she clamored out of bed, wishing she could just say where she was, and gathered the file from the desk.

Soon, she found herself in the music room downstairs. The one space that Roz designated as hers and Penny's—even though Penny barely used it. The piano bench in front of the shiny, black Baby Grand seemed like a good spot to get comfortable while she flipped open the file on her lap. Before long, she had music filtering through the speaker on her phone. A song she had composed when she was only thirteen, but one of her favorites.

If hating something could be called a favorite.

Every key—each rising note—resurrected her pain because she could remember in perfect detail just how much agony had filled her heart when she created the piece years ago. All of her music was like that. A lot like her past, too.

The music helped, though.

In some ways.

She was able to lose herself in the sound of the music, and the notes coloring up her mind, as she flipped page after page in the file. The information about the trust fund and restitution payment from her father was as overwhelming as confusing as she thought it would be.

Then again, it was also clear.

One hundred million dollars. Delivered after her eighteenth birthday. *Nine and a half more months*. If only money could solve the rest of her problems, then Penny wouldn't have any to bother her, right?

*Bullshit*.

Lost in the file, Penny didn't hear the footsteps outside the music room until a throat cleared. Her head snapped up, eyes wide, as her gaze landed on the man standing in the doorway. For a brief second, panic welled in her throat in the form of a lump that kept her air stuck in her windpipe.

It took a second …

And then another for her to calm. *Breathe*.

Luca Puzza raised a hand to wave; a silent hello before he said, "Hey, sorry. Didn't mean to scare you."

Roz's brother, and Naz's best friend, waited for her to reply. She didn't. It was kind of hard when her heart raced so fast beneath her ribcage that it felt like the organ was about to explode. Except it wasn't from fear, now.

She saw the man around every now and then. Of course, he came to visit his sister, and she was sure he worked with Naz, too. The guy was just … there. The thing was, Penny didn't know how to deal with Luca. He was always kind, gave her space, and never looked at her without a smile on his face.

A *handsome* smile, she'd noticed.

The same way she noticed that he had the most striking green-blue eyes, and a face carved by God. High, sharp cheekbones and a jawline to die for. The intensity in his expressions couldn't be matched, she thought. He was tall, but not lanky. With hands that looked like he knew how to work.

He was also twenty-four.

Or twenty-five?

What did it matter?

He was too old for her.

And she didn't understand why she noticed any of those things about him at all. It wasn't like the guy indulged her in conversation because *she* certainly didn't go out of her way to talk to him. She barely knew him at all.

She just … liked the way he looked.

It was a stupid crush she couldn't explain. One he didn't know existed, and she was fine with that. It needed to stay that way.

"You okay?" Luca asked, his grin warm and beautiful.

Penny swallowed hard, thinking, *no.* She suddenly didn't know how to talk when he was around and she hated that, too. "Fine—I'm fine."

"You sure?"

Not at all.

# *3.*

*Luca*

"FINE—I'm fine."

"You sure?" Luca asked.

Because the girl didn't look fine.

*At all.*

Her wide eyes looked like large, blue moons. Clear, like the color of freshly frozen ice, he thought. There was something haunted in her stare and while he couldn't see any fear staring back at him, he figured she must be. The tint of pink in her pale skin and the straightness of her back spoke of her discomfort at the very sight of his interruption.

Luca hadn't meant to be a shit.

The girl was like a kitten. Small-featured. Pretty. Skittish at the slightest provocation.

*Vulnerable.*

A beautiful, *terrified* kitten.

There was no denying the very sight of her could invoke all sorts of feelings from the people around her. From the way she used her long layers of white-blonde hair as a curtain to shut the world out to the dark clothing she drowned her figure in and kept hidden from view. She radiated an aura of distress constantly. He'd noticed it over the past few months that she'd been living with his friend and sister. Whenever he came over to visit Roz or Naz, it was hard to ignore the way Penny shrunk away from any visitors, not wanting to engage.

It was like a person couldn't stop themselves from wanting to help her. In any way they possibly could, too.

Luca wasn't an exception to the rule.

Especially not now when he was sure his surprise intrusion had upset her. Considering some of the things he knew about her past—regarding men, specifically—it wasn't a shock. It also caused his stomach to twist with guilt. The last thing he wanted was for her to think that she was in danger around him.

On the scale of good to bad, Luca fell on the latter end of the spectrum … on paper. Because of his raising, the family he was born into, and the last name attached to his legacy, he was who he was. Crime was crime, right? He also thought he wasn't entirely bad—he *did* have a moral compass, to some regard. He wasn't a fucking monster.

He should just leave the girl alone.

She still hadn't even replied to his question.

Instead, he at least wanted to try to make her comfortable before he got out of her sight. Luca grinned, saying, "Really, I'm sorry for scaring you. I didn't know anyone was home when Naz asked me to stop and grab something out of his office for him. I would have shouted at the front door to warn you had I known you were back here when I heard something this way."

Penny kept staring.

*Silent.*

She swallowed hard enough for him to hear it, though.

Shit.

He had freaked her out.

*Damn.*

Now he felt worse.

Luca wasn't even going to try to fix the situation when clearly, he wasn't doing a very good job in the first place. Jerking a thumb over his shoulder, the squeak of his leather jacket loud in the resounding quietness of the music room, he said, "I think it might be better if I just go, yeah? I'll see you later, Penny."

That said, he turned to leave.

Later, he could give Naz a heads up and apologize for whatever episode Penny might have because he was a dumbass. If she did … Naz said it happened sometimes. Usually because of school or therapy, but apparently anything could bring it on if the situation was stressful enough. Luca didn't know what those *episodes* entailed, but he hated the idea that he might cause one just by being there.

"The music," he heard blurted behind him, "it's mine."

Luca's shoulders tensed, his steps hesitating. "What?"

Softer, Penny explained, "The piano. You heard my music. But it's … mine. My composition."

Glancing over his shoulder, but not wanting to give the girl the impression he planned to stay when she was already uncomfortable, he said, "Oh."

Like a fool.

Just *oh.*

Quickly, he added, "The song is beautiful."

It had already stopped playing. Just shortly after he first interrupted whatever she was reading in the file on her lap, actually, but he didn't notice until then in the midst of everything.

The red tint in Penny's cheeks became deeper at his praise, and her gaze dropped down to the file in her lap. It caused a wave of her hair to drop in front of her face at the same time, but he was pretty sure he had seen the hint of a smile curving her full, soft pink lips before it was gone from sight.

Then, he heard her whispered, "Thanks."

He almost didn't.

It was so low.

She did lift her head again, but that time she wouldn't meet his gaze. Instead, opting to stare at anything else *but* him. The blush was still very present on her cheeks, and the smile was long gone, but at least, she wasn't hiding from him. Wasn't that a step forward?

He thought so.

Penny shrugged. The oversized, black hoodie that swallowed her body right down to her knees barely moved at all from the action. Her blue stare drifted to him, and only briefly met his gaze, before darting away just as fast. He could hear every awkward syllable when she told him, "Sorry—you probably think I'm a freak."

"Why would I think that?"

"Because I don't know how to talk to a gu—*you.* Anyone, really." Penny sighed, closing the folder in her lap before she added, "But my therapist keeps telling me that I should try to start conversations more even if I don't want to. It's the only way I'll learn how to … *talk*?"

Why did that sound like a question?

Luca didn't get the chance to ask.

"But I don't really know how to," she said, reverting back to the same soft tone as before that was quieter than a mouse skirting across the floor. "Talk, or start a conversation, I mean."

That made him smile.

He couldn't say that he didn't pity the girl—her situation before she came to live with his sister and best friend kind of made that hard. If anyone deserved pity and time to get their life straight, it was Penny.

"You don't give yourself enough credit," Luca said, winking her way when Penny's head snapped up, and those wide eyes nailed into him. "You're doing great—all things considered. One step at a time. One breath after another. Even if that's all you can do, you're doing it. You know?"

Penny blinked, but otherwise, offered nothing in reply.

Luca figured she deserved to know … "I'm not going to pretend to know your life or the shit you're going through, but from what I do know … hell, you get out of bed, Penny. You're alive. *Trying.* You know that's all Naz and Roz ask of you, right? Just that you try. They're willing to do whatever you need so that you can keep trying."

It took her a second.

Eventually, she murmured, "Yeah, I know."

"And that song—I think it would be awesome if you played it in a minor key, or at least the last stanza." Luca grinned, waving a hand when he added, "But I don't know shit about music. Not like Roz or you, anyway."

That made her laugh.

*Really* laugh.

A genuine sound that had her young face lighting up in such a way that it was impossible for Luca to tear his gaze away when she dared to toss her head back as the amusement radiated from her. She was too beautiful of a creature to be constantly sad, but he couldn't help but wonder … how long it had been since she laughed like she just did?

She should do that more often. He hoped that eventually, she might be able to find someone who made her laugh like he just had. *Again and again.* Everybody deserved someone to make them happy.

Luca would have said more, but the buzz of his phone stopped him. Pulling the device from the pocket of his dark-wash jeans, the same ones his father had bitched about the blown-out knees the last time Zeke saw him wearing them, he checked the messages.

One from Naz waited.

*Did you grab the file from my office yet?*

Right.

The entire reason he was here. He didn't regret agreeing to help Naz out more than he already did while his friend needed it, but shit … Luca didn't stop running. If he didn't have time for his college obligations before, he sure as hell didn't have time for them now.

Raising his phone for Penny to see, Luca offered an apologetic expression when he said, "Sorry, I gotta grab something for Naz and head out before he comes looking for me. You good?"

Penny smiled.

It seemed real.

"Yeah, Luca. I'm good. Thanks."

"No problem."

And he meant it.

On his way out of the house with the file in hand, Luca heard the echo of the same song that greeted him when he entered the house. Only now, she played it in a minor key.

• • •

Luca arrived at Dizzy's to find Naz had situated himself at the bar where he could enjoy a glass of whiskey while he finished up a phone call. He only heard the tail end of the conversation as he approached and took the stool next to his friend.

"Can't say we're going to make it happen that soon, *Zio*," Naz said into the phone, "but I'll let Dad know and see if he wants to go with Chicago for that offer. You know how he is … *yeah*, it's all about that bottom dollar. Later."

"Chicago, huh?" Luca asked when Naz ended the call and tossed the phone to the bar top. "Donatis are making deals with Chicago?"

"Occasionally. Depends on the—"

"Money."

Naz grinned. "This business is all about money. Even when it's family."

*Right.*

Luca wouldn't forget it.

Turning so his back faced the bar and he could observe the empty club, Luca rested his elbows on the edge. The folder he had grabbed for Naz hung from his fingertips, waiting to be passed over. A lot could be done to the club to spruce it up and make it a bit more … *seemly*. Especially for a business that Naz used on a regular basis. Yet, his friend purchased the club over a year ago and had yet to make any effort to get the place up to the standard of his name.

"You ever gonna get this place *Donati* ready?" Luca asked, knowing Naz would understand what he meant well enough.

Naz scoffed under his breath. "Why?"

"I don't know. Maybe a place you frequent regularly *and* own should actually look like you own it. Right now, it looks better fit for the dregs."

"It's fine for me."

Luca shifted his gaze Naz's way. "Is it?"

Naz only shrugged. "Despite how some people in our business like to present themselves to the rest of the world, I'm fine being exactly who I am. If that makes me stand out amongst the crowd, so be it. I'm not the standard, Luca. I am the exception. *Exceptional*."

Luca grinned.

He couldn't help it.

That was the same shit their fathers had been telling them for years in regards to the family business. They didn't have to follow the rules—they *were* the fucking rules. If only Luca could apply that same philosophy to everything else in his life, shit would be grand.

Right?

"And knock that shit off," Naz muttered, rolling his eyes Luca's way. "You sound like your father when you mouth off like that, you know?"

Yeah.

*Shit.*

"Here."

He slapped the folder in front of his friend, but Naz didn't bother to reach for it when he muttered around the rim of his glass, "Thanks. Saved me the time of driving out of the city just to pick it up. You'd think I might have my shit together by now, but—"

"We're all doing what we can."

Naz chuckled and set the glass back to the bar. "Yeah, tell me about it.

Between Roz being pregnant … Dad piling on more shit for me with business, and everything else, I don't know what I'm doing half the time. Supposed to be a genius here, but I can't even remember a fucking file I put right on my desk, so I wouldn't forget it this morning. Some shit, that."

Luca couldn't help but notice how Naz didn't mention Penny amongst the stress in his life. That also reminded him that he should probably let his friend know about the run-in he had with the girl at the house.

"Penny was at the house, by the way," Luca said.

Next to him, Naz nodded. "Skipped school again, probably."

"Again?"

Naz didn't seem concerned when he explained, "Sometimes, she makes it a whole day. Other times, she barely makes it through the front doors before she turns back around. I pay enough money to the school that they … overlook small infractions."

"Does Roz know—"

"She's the one who told Penny not to push it. If shit isn't good for her, then she doesn't need to be stressing out over something like *classes*. She's got enough going on. We give her the freedom she needs to work through it. What else can we do?"

"Yeah, I guess."

Naz sighed, scrubbing a hand over his face. "My shit seems small in comparison. I mean, her father was just sentenced, and the lawyers are pressuring everyone to finish the paperwork needed for the asshole's estate and restitution payments. Imagine, Luca, the man who raped and sold you to others for them to do the same is basically handing you millions of dollars … a way to *apologize*. Like that shit should *fix* what he did to her. I'm surprised when she does make the effort to get up and go to school, honestly."

Luca swallowed the uncomfortable lump in his throat, thinking about Penny at the house all alone. Hell, should she even *be* alone? That was the real question. Was there too much freedom for the girl in her situation?

He didn't know.

"Do you ever think," Luca asked his friend, "that if you give someone too much rope … they might just hang themselves with it?"

Naz lifted his brow and reached for the glass with a mouthful of liquor left in the bottom. He drained what remained of the whiskey, and then muttered heavily, "All the fucking time, man. All the time."

# 4.

*Penny*

*CLICK, click, clack, click, clack, click, click.*

Penny blinked, bleary-eyed and still tired, as she climbed down the dark stairwell of the suburban house where she had called home for the last several months. Maybe it had been the trip to her therapist yesterday evening, but she'd had a train of nightmares since falling asleep, and she just wasn't in the mood to try again.

But what was that sound?

Penny found the source of the late-night noise soon enough. "What are you doing?"

The man on the couch stiffened, and just as quickly, shot a look over his shoulder at her. Reaching up, he was quick to close the laptop he'd been leaning over the coffee table to type on. "Nothing. What are you doing out of bed?"

"Can't sleep. Usually, when people say nothing they don't also feel the need to hide their computer screens, you know?"

Penny had a love-slash-hate relationship with the internet, and computers. She was like every sixteen-year-old girl who seemed to find too much self-worth on social media, and that was how she preferred to connect with people she wanted to keep in her life. It was easier than trying in real life because that always ended badly.

She had no friends in her new, private high school. She had a few hundred on her socials.

It just didn't have to be deep.

But in the same breath, she hated the internet for many reasons. On certain places in the dark web, one could find folders upon folders of photos of her that were up for sale. Ranging from the age of one, up until she was almost thirteen. Those photos had not yet fallen into hands that could distribute them beyond the dark web where it would touch the people in her real life, but it all still felt a little too real to her.

And raw.

Sometimes, her life felt like a time bomb that was constantly ticking down. Someday—maybe—those photos would find their way out into the world. Penny wasn't fucking stupid, she knew how horrible people could be. They wouldn't care that she was a child trafficking victim. They wouldn't care that those photos were proof of her sexual abuse. All they would see, for the slightly older ones, were a young girl showing her body to a camera.

She hoped they never saw the light of day.

Naz sighed, and then chuckled. "Maybe you're not wrong, then, but that doesn't mean it's any of your business about what I was doing, either."

"Fair enough." Penny crossed around the couch and dropped into the recliner across from where Naz was sitting. "So, what are you hiding?"

"You think I would tell you?"

"Why not?"

"You know, I think this is the longest conversation we've had since you moved in with us months ago, Penny."

She had to think about it, but it didn't take her very long at all to realize that he wasn't exaggerating. She blinked, trying to pull something out of her zipped lips to say that would be appropriate. All she managed to settle on was, "I didn't know there was a me for a long time—I didn't have a voice to use."

Naz nodded. "I know, I didn't take it personally."

"You know I like you, right?"

He raised his brows. "Oh?"

Penny shrugged. "I haven't tried to ruin your life yet—that's good sign number one."

"That's not funny."

"And that doesn't make it less true, either."

Naz made a noise under his breath. "All right."

"Now that all the deflections are past us," Penny said with a smile and a wave of her hand between them, "what are you hiding?"

Because he was, she knew.

Penny just had that sense—she looked at people, and she could tell when they were lying, or if they were someone who might hurt her. Naz didn't fall into the hurt category. Like Roz, all he ever did was try to help her, but in his own way. Sometimes, that meant giving her space, and letting her figure out whatever she needed on her own time. She appreciated that more than he could possibly know.

Rarely did people leave her alone.

Naz sighed loudly. "You tell me."

Flipping open the laptop, he turned it around on the table so Penny could see what was on the screen … which wasn't anything that made sense to her. A bunch of letters and numbers and symbols on a white screen, filling it from side to side.

It looked like … HTML?

But more.

"Is that code?" Penny asked.

"Good call," Naz returned.

"You write code?"

Naz lifted one shoulder like it wasn't a big thing. "I do a little bit of everything, it's how my brain focuses."

Right.

Over the last few months, Penny had heard more than one person refer to Naz as a literal genius. She had seen enough of his whiteboards filled with formulas that she didn't understand around their house to know he was smart.

He was also more.

He left early in the morning—drove a black car and wore a suit. Words like *family business* and *made man* were thrown around in low tones like Penny wouldn't be able to hear if they spoke quietly. Which was crap, because she did hear. And because she had access to the internet, she looked that shit up.

Apparently, Naz's family, and Roz's … well, they were criminals. Not the kind of criminals that hurt Penny, but criminals under the law, anyway. And they had been that way for a long time. Penny never asked about it, she didn't think the details of what the internet told her where mafia families had reigned in New York for years was something she really needed to understand, but here she was.

"What's the code for?" Penny asked.

Naz sucked air through his teeth. "That's … a harder answer."

"Why?"

"Because."

"That's a non-answer."

Naz gave her a look. "I just don't think I should talk—"

"Is it about the mafia?"

He kept staring at her, expression unmovable. "And what do you know about that?"

"What I found on the internet."

"That shit lies."

"But does it really?"

Naz's cheek twitched. "Are we talking about this code or the fucking mafia?"

"You're not a very good liar, are you?"

"Not to people I care about, no."

*Huh.*

He cared about her.

Penny peeked at the screen. "Is it going to run something?"

"Yes, a program."

"That does what?"

"Crawls the dark web, the public internet, and government servers, so long as they don't detect it. It'll cross countries, it'll even break through the secure internet protections countries like China has that they use to monitor and control their citizens."

Penny's brow dipped. "But why?"

"That's the hard part."

"Why?"

Naz straightened and folded his hands over his knees as he stared at her. "You told Roz there was a network of people involved in the … thing your father was doing. Right?"

Penny swallowed hard. "So what?"

"When the police asked you for more information about that, you went quiet."

"Because look what they did with my father."

"Right," Naz said, "but there are still people out there, Penny … hurting kids."

"And?"

"This program is going to catch them—or at the very least, identify them, and then gather evidence of their business on the dark web, which will then be compiled into zipped, protected files before being delivered to whichever law enforcement is closest to their areas."

She blinked.

That sounded … "That's impossible."

"No, it isn't. I had a base program to work off—one that was made decades ago called Thorn. It crawled the dark web looking for child porn, which it would then try to match using facial recognition and other landmarks, should the photos include those, to real children. The problem was, that was a white hat system. It only worked legally. It didn't go over the line into the gray, or outright black, sides of hacking on the dark web. So, it had limitations. Mine does not, and since it will run constantly without me needing to touch it, and as I have it going through so many servers that it'll never be traced back to me. Or rather, it would take them a very long time to figure out it was me.

"This program will hack into government databases, into school databases. It will pull pictures of children from online yearbooks, and teachers from school websites. It will pull criminal records, and it will look into workers whose photos are on the internet. I have a friend who is also working with a guy that runs a program which hacks into every single security camera that runs on Wi-Fi, which means at some point, it will also be able to just—"

"Run through faces from the general public," Penny said faintly.

Naz nodded and pointed at the laptop. "That was the last bit of code needed. All I have to do now is hit that black button where it says RUN in the left-hand corner, and the system will be live in the dark web."

"Can't other people detect it, or—"

"Highly unlikely, given the way it was designed."

"Don't the people using the dark web have things to protect—"

"It's going to hack into those systems, too. It'll create small wormholes that will be virtually undetectable, which will suck in their coded information, before running through it to decode as much of it as it possibly can. That will leave the program with information of the people behind the forums."

Holy shit.

"I know it doesn't change what's already happened," Naz murmured, "and it's not going to make your life better or easier to get through what's been done to you, Penny, but it's going to help someone else. It's going to save someone else. Nobody gets to change the past—we can only change the future."

"Yeah …"

"The code is finished. You can press the black button, if you'd like."

She stared at the screen for a while.

Naz waited her out.

Then, without warning, Penny leaned forward, and hit the RUN button. The screen blinked, the white background turning black as the words turned white and began to scroll. It was almost beautiful, really.

"I still wish he was dead," Penny muttered.

"I can make that happen, too."

Naz said it so flippantly.

That's how she knew he wasn't lying.

"But would you?" she asked quietly.

"You should watch the news more often," Naz said instead, "I hear you learn a lot from it."

What did that even mean?

He didn't give her the chance to ask.

"How many names of people do you know that can be tied to this ring your father was involved in?"

"Not many. I rarely got their names."

"But some," he pressed.

"A few," she whispered.

"Would you write them down for me?"

Penny glanced over at him. "Why?"

"Sometimes, we just don't get what we want from the law, Penny."

Well …

He wasn't wrong.

• • •

"Miss Dunsworth, what is the square root of—"

"Pass," Penny muttered.

"You can't just pass a question because you don't want to answer it, Penny."

She sighed. "Pass."

Light laughter filtered through the classroom, but Penny was more interested in staring out the window. She would much rather do her studies online, or even with a tutor at home, but the chick who came around every once in a while to check in on Penny, and her living situation being fostered with Roz and Naz said it would be better for her to be in school.

With people.

Yuck.

The only good thing about this hell was the fact that Roz had allowed Penny to pick what school she wanted to attend, and then Naz came in to drop a whole bunch of money to make sure Penny had just enough freedom to breathe here.

Like now.

Sticking her hand up, the teacher's gaze drifted to her. "Yes?"

"I want to go see Mrs. Canns."

The school counselor.

The teacher's lips pursed like she was considering refusing Penny's request, but the woman eventually nodded with a jerk of her thumb toward the door. It took Penny no time at all to pack up her shit, and head out of the classroom, leaving the rest of the teenaged idiots behind her. She was only here because she needed to be—she needed a fucking diploma.

That was it.

She didn't have friends.

Didn't want them.

No one here would ever understand Penny, or her life. She was the weird one—the freak. In gym, they noticed she only wore long sleeve shirts, and black leggings. And so, the rumors about what she was hiding under her clothes started. Not that they were wrong, she just didn't care to indulge them. The group of High Bitches in Charge and their Merry Band of Fucktoys for boys made it their mission to piss Penny off at least once a day, and that was a feat.

You know, considering Penny felt nothing.

Most of the time.

She didn't go to the counselor. Instead, she headed outside through an exit door, and pulled a small metal case from her bag. Flipping it open, she found a handful of cigarettes, and two joints. She'd save the weed for later … maybe.

Roz didn't like it.

Naz didn't have an opinion.

It soothed her mind.

It was the only time she didn't have to think.

Lighting up a cigarette, Penny let the smoke soak into her lungs as she stared out over the west side of the parking lot. No doubt, the school already had her on camera coming out to smoke, and someone was on their way to drag her back inside. Security, likely.

She didn't want to go back in there.

She didn't want to be here at all.

And not just here … but here.

*Alive.*

Breathing.

On earth.

That was when Penny realized her depression was back, and better than ever. It wasn't like it had gone away, really, but it became far more manageable over the last year. She didn't know what it was like to live without depression. At three years old, she had her first moment of suicidal ideation. Here she was at seventeen, and she was still looking out at the road thinking … how easy would it be to just run out in front of traffic?

Fucking bitch.

Yeah, that's exactly what depression was.

A goddamn bitch.

"Penny Dunsworth, get back inside the school right now!"

Penny sighed.

*Figures.*

She didn't do as the security guard told her. Instead, she stood, slinging her messenger bag and purse over her shoulder before she darted into the parking lot without a look over her shoulder. She didn't have a car here—still didn't know how to drive.

Not that it mattered.

She didn't mind a walk.

Penny just didn't know what she was walking toward anymore.

• • •

"Do you ever work?"

Naz didn't look the least bit surprised to see Penny standing in the doorway of their living room. "Do you ever stay at school like you're supposed to?"

"Bad day."

"Idiots again, or …?"

Penny shrugged. "Bad thoughts."

That was her way of letting them know without saying something about her depression. She kind of felt like it was a check on herself, in a way. If other people knew she was having dark thoughts, she was less likely to act on them with self-harm, or something of a similar nature. It didn't always work, but it helped.

Especially with Naz and Roz.

They didn't judge.

Naz folded his arms behind his head and eyed her from the side. "I do work, actually. And do you know what else I do?"

"Not particularly."

"Get phone calls from the school when you skip out. I figured you would be coming home, so I said I would be there to meet you. I should be on the other side of the city, though."

Huh.

"Where's Roz?"

"You have to stop skipping school."

"I would if I could do it online."

Naz lifted a brow. "You're supposed to socialize. It's a good thing to learn."

"I do. With you, Roz, and people around here. That school is annoying."

"Is it, or is it—"

"I hate that school, and the people in it."

"You chose that school."

Penny rolled her eyes so hard it hurt. "Because I had to."

Naz pursed his lips. "Two days at the school, three days at home online."

"Oh, we're bartering now?"

"Everybody gets something they want."

"What will the social worker say?"

"Fuck her," Naz said, "her shit doesn't work, anyway."

*Well …*

He had a point.

"Two days there, three here," she agreed.

Naz nodded, clearly pleased. "You only have a few months left to go before you graduate. At least try to make it until then."

"Yeah, but then what happens?"

He was silent.

Penny, too.

"Well," he finally said quietly, "that's the beauty of it. You can do whatever you want."

But could she?

*Could she really?*

"I don't … know what I want," she admitted.

Naz gave her another look from the side. "Yeah, I imagine that's a big part of the problem, huh?"

More than he knew.

Penny didn't understand her purpose.

Why was she even alive?

"And you didn't answer me—where is Roz?"

"Getting a massage right about now. She worries all the time. About the baby, me … you. She rarely even takes time to play the piano lately. So, I set up a day for her to relax, and nothing more. Which is why I am here right now, and she is not."

"Are we going to tell her I skipped again?"

Naz scowled. "Probably not."

"I'll try to do better."

She expected a *but will you?*

Instead, he smiled. "The best you can do is all we ask for, Penny."

Yeah, she knew.

It's why she was still here.

That, and … "Did you guys pick a name yet?"

"We were thinking Cross, for my father."

"I like it."

"Roz is going to ask you to be a godmother."

Well, then.

Penny just blinked.

Naz said nothing as he pushed up from the couch until he came to stand in front of her. "And I thought you would like to know, before someone calls and tells you."

"Know what?"

"Yesterday, your father was found murdered in the prison kitchen. Apparently, he washed dishes to earn privileges. They're not really sure what happened … but dental records confirmed the identity this morning."

Penny stilled.

Naz let her have the moment.

She almost wanted to ask if he did it. But how? He'd said he could make it happen, after all.

A part of her wanted to have a breakdown right then and there. Her fragile mental state could never be trusted to handle something like this. Another part of her felt a sick sort of glee to know one of her monsters—one of her biggest demons—was dead. The rest of her felt nothing at all, but that wasn't unusual.

An old friend, really.

Penny decided to ask, "Do you think God forgave him for what he did to me?"

Naz considered that. "I don't know."

"Well, I never will."

"I'm sure he died knowing that."

Good.

It's what he deserved.

# 5.

*Luca*

ARRIVING late to a family dinner wasn't anything unusual for Luca, lately. Running like a crazy man for Naz made it hard to be on time, not that anyone complained when he slid into his usual chair at his mother's dining room table long after the food had been served.

Katya didn't seem to mind when she beamed at him from her end of the table. Shit, there was a first time for everything. "I'll grab you a plate, Luca."

He knew better than to tell her to stay where she was—he was a grown man and was capable of fixing his own plate, but that wouldn't matter to Katya. Guests that came for dinner at her home did very little but talk and eat.

Still, he tried.

"I can get it in a minute, Ma," he told her.

Katya raised a brow. "I will. You sit."

*Right.*

As he expected.

Katya left her chair and had to pass his to exit the dining room into the kitchen. On her way by, she patted the top of his head like one might do to a puppy. Except it didn't bother him all that much. The fondness in his mother's action was familiar and comforting in a way a lot of things weren't for him. He might very well be a grown man, but he still adored his mom to the ends of the earth and back.

Even if sometimes, she drove him crazy.

Luca tried rejoining the conversation happening at the table. Or rather, get caught up on what Roz and Naz were chatting about with Penny and his father. Zeke, to his benefit, was only occasionally jumping in with something to say while Luca's sister and Naz were doing the bulk of the work throughout the conversation with Penny.

He hadn't seen her in a month, but she didn't look … any different, he supposed. In her case, he wasn't sure if that was a good or bad thing, all things considered. She was still wearing a sweater that was at least five sizes too big but hey, it wasn't black. It also wasn't any color that would make her stand out either. The flat gray sweater with a logo on the front was a step up from her usual black, though. He had to give her that. She was still using her hair as a curtain between herself and anyone else that she didn't want to converse with.

That just happened to be his father at the moment. Not that Zeke seemed very concerned with Penny's attempt to distance herself from him.

For a brief second, Penny's gaze lifted to find Luca sitting across from her at the table. A welcoming smile stretched his mouth; it was the only way he could seem encouraging when it was obvious she was starting to get uncomfortable.

The girl barely left the house. He was positive she hadn't sat at his parents' dinner table before now. Naz admitted to him the week before that trying to get Penny to do anything that involved other people was like pulling teeth.

In some ways, he understood that—*her*. He didn't always want to engage, either. That didn't change the fact he still had to and so he did. They all had to do shit they didn't want to. It was a part of life.

But …

Her life hadn't been like theirs, either. Maybe it wasn't fair of him to assume that she should behave the same way the rest of them did just because it's what everyone else did.

Katya returned to the dining room with Luca's plate in hand. She placed the ravioli casserole mess in front of him with a smile.

"Thanks. Ma."

"Eat up," she told him. "And there's more if you want it."

Oh, he would.

No doubt.

There was nothing quite like his mother's cooking after he spent a day running from one side of the city to the other. The saucy pasta goodness flooded his mouth as the conversation picked up with Katya rejoining the table.

"Have we decided on something yet?" she asked once she was back in her chair. "I still think we should do the party thing. It's only fair, Penny."

Luca glanced up, still not entirely caught up on the conversation that had been happening before he even arrived. He knew it had something to do with Penny simply because of the way the attention at the table continued going back to her, but everyone seemed to want to tiptoe around whatever topic they were trying to discuss.

His mother didn't have the couth for that. She was never one to beat around the bush. Not when she had something to say and the time to say it, anyway.

"You didn't even let Roz throw you a party for your seventeenth birthday months ago." Despite Katya's kind smile leveling on Penny from the other end of the table from the teenage girl, it wasn't working to encourage anything. Penny settled on tipping her head down and using her fork to push around what remained on her plate while not even entertaining the idea of replying to Luca's mother. Katya didn't appear offended, instead saying, "Your graduation and eighteenth birthday are right around the same time—within a few weeks, anyway. Why not just let us throw you something for both? One party instead of two."

"We're still trying to figure out the details," Roz put in when Penny stayed silent. "Right, Penny?"

The girl only shrugged.

That did make Luca's mom frown.

Katya's gaze darted down the table to where Zeke sat sipping on a glass of red wine as if she was trying to get *him* to engage Penny alongside her. His father continued to drink his wine like he had nothing better to do at the moment.

How long had they been at this with Penny?

Too long, apparently.

"Excuse me," Penny muttered, standing from the table without warning. She didn't even bother to explain why she was leaving the table—a sign of disrespect at an Italian family's table if there ever was one—before she headed out of the dining room without a look over her shoulder.

Roz sighed at the exit. "Well, that's that."

"Sorry," Naz said to Katya. "Sometimes she's just … not in the mood. She was up for dinner today, but I don't think she's ready to talk parties and everything else."

"I get it," his mother murmured.

She seemed fine.

Luca wondered if Katya really was.

"The more you push, the easier it is for her to move away."

All eyes at the table turned on Luca at his seemingly random statement. But hell, if anyone had been paying attention, it wouldn't *be* random. Nothing about Penny screamed approachable or willing … yet, people seemed to think they could change that about her if only they tried harder.

It wouldn't happen.

Not unless she wanted it to.

He also knew why his family kept trying to get Penny to open up. They cared enough to do anything at all. He doubted it came across that way to her, though. When all someone wanted to do was disappear, being *seen* wasn't exactly a good thing.

Then, Luca pointed at the food on his plate and grinned at his mother, saying, "But this is delicious, Ma. Really."

Katya beamed again. "Thank you."

At least, one thing was okay.

Luca could handle that.

Later, when his mother was distracted with clearing the table and the topic of Roz's pregnancy, Luca slipped away from the table knowing he wouldn't be missed. At least, not for a few minutes. It was all he needed.

He found Penny in the entry hall sitting on the stairs. With her back to the white railing, she wasn't even pretending to be busy while she picked at her fingernails and avoided his stare as he leaned against the wall. That was fine—he didn't mind that she wanted to ignore him. It wouldn't stop him from saying what he was there to say.

"They care, you know?" Luca shrugged when Penny dared to glance upward at him. "That's why my mom tries to start a conversation with you or why my dad forces himself to talk even though he's not the type. They've already let you *in*—in the family sense. You wouldn't be here otherwise. But now they're trying to get you in, too."

Penny didn't reply.

Luca continued, anyway. "I think you've been around long enough now to know that we're not the type of people who allow outsiders in. We just … can't afford to, Penny. But they do with you because again, *they care*."

"Well, they shouldn't."

Finally, a response.

Not that it was one he liked.

*Beggars can't be choosers.*

"I'm not worth that," Penny muttered after a moment. "I'm not worth very much at all."

*Shit.*

Luca knew that feeling all too well. He was still trying to deal with it, but that didn't change the fact that feeling worthless wasn't the same as actually *being* worthless to the people who loved him. Maybe that was the biggest difference between him and Penny. His self-doubt was created in his own mind while hers had been taught. He didn't think they could unlearn it in the same ways, either.

"Not that you need me to say it, because I'm sure everybody else points it out more than enough," Luca said, folding his arms over his chest while he eyed the family portrait hanging opposite to the stairwell, "but you know that isn't true."

"Feels like it."

"Rough week?"

Penny scoffed.

*Hard.*

"Rough life," she mumbled.

Yeah, he bet.

Penny went back to fidgeting with her fingernails and then the sleeves of her sweater. She made a great effort to keep every inch of her skin covered, but she tugged at the wrist band of the sleeve just enough for him to notice the patchwork of scars that started there and seemed to keep going beneath the gray fabric where he couldn't see.

Luca should look away.

He didn't.

Naz mentioned she was a cutter but hadn't gone into details. The respect of the matter, really, and Luca understood. Still, he couldn't help but wonder how far those scars went … how many did she have? Had she stopped cutting yet?

Eventually, she noticed his staring.

"Stop it," Penny told him.

Luca raised a brow. "Why? I'm just looking."

Penny quickly fixed the sleeve of her sweater, hiding the scars in a flash. "Don't pity me."

"I don't." Then just as fast, he corrected himself with, "I don't anymore. I did at first. And it's not that I think you don't deserve my pity, but more that I don't think you want it. Why pity someone who doesn't want it when that won't help, right?"

She met his stare.

Luca only smiled back.

What else could he do?

What could *any* of them do for her other than smile and keep saying shit would get better? It was easier said than done, but it also wasn't a lie.

"And stop that, too," she whispered.

Luca arched a brow. "What?"

"The staring."

"I—"

"You don't look at me the same way everyone else does. Like they're scared of me—or the idea of me. I like that."

Luca blinked, unsure of what she was saying. "You like that people are scared of you or that I don't see you the same way they do?"

Penny stood up from the stairs quick enough that he had to move when she passed him at the bottom of the stairs. It wasn't fast enough that he hadn't been able to see the pink tint coloring her cheeks even though she wouldn't meet his gaze on the way by.

He still managed to hear her say, "*You.* I like you. And I don't know what to do about that."

Then, she was gone around the corner.

Luca was left confused.

He heard what she said.

Perfectly clear.

And he could still see the blush staining her cheeks even though she was long gone from his presence.

*You.*

*I like you.*

Did she mean …

It didn't matter.

Luca couldn't entertain that thought.

He wouldn't.

• • •

"Even if you were late," Luca's mother told him after she walked him to the front door when he was leaving, "I'm still happy you showed up."

Luca grinned.

It was the first time she even mentioned the fact he was late for dinner. As was Katya's usual way.

"I'll try to be on time for the next one," he replied, kissing the apple of her cheek. "How's that?"

"Better. *And*."

"Hmm?"

Luca reached for the coat he'd left hanging on a hook in the hallway. Shrugging the item on while his mother glanced behind herself down the entry hall as though she were looking for someone who might be listening, he waited for whatever she had to tell him. He also wasn't known for his patience.

"And what, Ma?"

Katya's attention came back to him in an instant. "Penny. Thank you for … talking to her. Everyone else seems fine to let her shrink away in the corner if that's what she wants. You make an effort to actually *talk*. It does make a difference."

He stiffened. "Did you follow me—"

"I went to check on *her*, actually. I thought I might have made her uncomfortable, and I don't want her to feel that way around any of us. She's important to your sister, you know?"

He did.

Too well.

"I don't think she means to be rude," Luca said about Penny, and stuffing his hands into his pockets. "But I don't think she knows how to deal with … people, either."

For a brief while, his mother only stared at him, saying nothing. Her palm came up to find his cheek with a soft pat that had him smiling.

"She's not rude. She's hurting."

"That, too," he murmured. "But I don't know … she said something to me earlier, and it made me think."

"About?"

"If I should be talking to her at all."

Katya frowned. "Did she tell you to leave her alone or—"

"Not quite."

His mother said nothing.

Luca sighed, admitting, "I think she might have a crush on me. Silly, right? I just … she's only seventeen, and I don't want her to think I'm encouraging any—"

"Imagine," Katya interjected, "what it must feel like to be the girl everyone knows was raped. Every person who looks at you knows *that* about you first. The one fact they do know is that you're a victim. It creates a complex in your head almost … every time you walk into a room, and people look at you, even if you don't know them, you wonder if that's the first thing on their mind. *Your* rape. Your constant victimhood."

He swallowed hard, taking in his mother's words. If anyone could relate to Penny at her current stage, it would be his mom. Before she came to be his father's wife, she had been the property of a man who used her and her body as he saw fit. He allowed others to do the same to Katya without regret or regard for her.

Yet, she survived.

She was amazing.

Katya didn't relent, adding, "It's going to take time for Penny to *be* Penny without feeling like that is also a part of her identity. Maybe it'll take months. It could be years. It might be something that never really goes away, either. She will, however, learn how to deal with it. The rest of us shouldn't treat her differently while she does it. That won't help. She doesn't *want* to be different, Luca."

Fair.

But …

"How does that have anything to do with me or what I said?"

Katya smiled. "Because she is still a *woman*."

"No, she's a girl."

"*No*, she's a young woman, Luca. And just because she's also a victim and a survivor doesn't change that while she's dealing with her recovery, she's also going through the same things every seventeen-year-old woman does. She feels the same things. Does the same things. Even if she's doing them in her own way. That includes … *you*."

"What?"

"Boys. *Men*. Noticing they exist. It's just a little more complicated for her … it has to be considering the circumstances. She talks to you, though," Katya said, shrugging. "Which at the very least, means she thinks you're safe to do that with. *Talk*. Like you. You don't have to do anything other than that, and I don't expect you to. You know how to behave."

"Huh."

"There are men in the world that teach women monsters do exist, but then there are other men who help us learn that not every man is one. If you're already safe to her, don't be someone who proves her wrong. I'm sure she's had enough that have."

*Yeah.*

He bet.

# 6.

*Penny*

WHY did things always have to get worse before they got better? Penny didn't have the answer, and nothing was looking up for her lately, so the *better* part of her equation wasn't coming anytime soon. That was never more apparent to her than while she sat in the principal's office at her private school while the woman currently sitting on the other side of the large desk went over every infraction against Penny since she starting attending the institution.

Before, skipping a day—or *several* in the same week—hadn't been a problem. Neither was her leaving classes early or her lack of interest in participating with the rest of the students. But then things started to get worse, her teachers started speaking up more, and the principal stopped overlooking what she called *the obvious*.

Or rather, Penny's issues.

"Need I return to the topic of her delinquency again?" Mrs. Tippens asked. "Do you know how many days she's missed this semester alone? And that's before we even get into the half days, or the showing up late … random missed classes in the middle of the day! Her attendance is the worst for any student on record at this school."

"She has good and bad days," Naz returned, unbothered by the principal's show of irritation. "Given the circumstances around Penny before she came here, I thought we both understood that there were times she wouldn't—or couldn't—attend simply because … well, we're not going into all that again. You were agreeable."

"Before I knew she was going to miss over half the year!" Mrs. Tippens fell back in the chair behind the desk and massaged her forehead with the pads of her fingers. "I was willing to work with the needs of my student—as I would for *any* student, Mr. Donati. I did not realize, however, the extent of Penny's …"

Needs?

Issues?

*Total fucking mess?*

She had a million descriptions to give the principal to help the woman out in her argument with Naz. Every single one of them would be valid, too, but she opted to not say anything at all. *Surprise.* The school was just another place starting to understand that things with Penny were not as easy as they seemed on the surface. Everyone saw her and what they knew on paper, and thought … *troubled.* Anyone could deal with a troubled teen.

They were idiots.

Penny was far beyond troubled.

She passed that years ago.

Mrs. Tippens sighed, murmuring, "At the time, I didn't fully comprehend the help and support Penny would need while attending this institution and finishing her final year. But it's also hard to come up with a proper plan to make sure she has what she needs when she doesn't even attend in the first place. I'm sure you understand."

Despite being uncomfortable in the chair and not wanting to be there in the first place, Penny had done so because Naz asked her. Now, she couldn't help rolling her eyes. Almost hard enough that she was able to see the back of her head. "You wouldn't want me here on my bad days."

"We want you here on all the days, Penny."

Next to her in the second chair that faced the large, modern desk, Naz cleared his throat and shot Penny a look. One that said she should be quiet, and *damn*, she was trying, but this was harder than she expected.

Leaning forward in his chair, Naz rested his arms over his knees and clasped his hands together. The smile he offered to the woman on the other side of the desk was kind. Friendly, even, but Penny knew that was all for show. If there was anything she learned about Naz over the many months she had been living under his roof, it was that he could appear like anything he wanted … or rather, what someone else wanted him to be.

Right then, the principal wanted compliance. An apology, maybe. She wanted Naz to tell her that everything would be handled from Penny's lack of interest in school to the grades that were barely passable.

She wanted him to lie.

Because shit … Penny planned on fixing nothing. This entire place was the least of her worries when it came to things she needed to handle in her life. Considering she still wasn't even happy to wake up each morning, why would she care about something as stupid as *high school*?

It seemed … ridiculous.

"The delinquency needs correcting," the principal said. "Fast and *first.* Then, we can maybe move to making other things better. Like engaging her peers, the issues with her teachers … incomplete schoolwork. All of it."

"And we're what, ignoring how difficult the last few months have been for her all the while?" Naz asked.

"I—"

"Her father's trial and then death. Her frail mental health. I think it's obvious that Penny does well to hold it together *visually*," Naz stressed, arching a brow as if to dare the woman across from him to deny his statement, "but where she struggles internally, we see it in things like her disinterest in other people, or the ability to finish tasks that takes a certain level of commitment and even enjoyment that she just doesn't *have*. Which I know you're aware because the school has a direct line to her therapist in case things come up that need to be handled … on either end. Is it really her fault for doing what she can, considering?"

"Mr. Donati—"

"Is it her fault?" he asked again, stronger the second time. "At least answer me."

Mrs. Tippens' gaze darted to Penny before moving right back to Naz. "My point is only that maybe this isn't the best place for her because it's become apparent we don't have the system in place for someone with Penny's needs. There are other places I could suggest that are better equipped to handle her delicate situation. Or a program, maybe, I—"

"What, like a ward?" Penny asked suddenly, the anger ringing out in every word. She glanced over at Naz, her brow pinched when she demanded, "Does she mean like a place they put me in overseas? Another hospital or—"

"That's not going to happen," Naz told her.

His tone was firm.

Other than Roz, only Naz or the social worker—if her guardians weren't doing their part in caring for her—could check her into another mental institution. She had to trust when he said it wasn't on the table, but a part of her still didn't believe it.

Penny still couldn't help the heaviness settling in her chest or the ache in her heart. That vicious swell of anxiety threatened to drown her under the rush of waves crashing into her one after the other with no end in sight. The way her mood could go from bleak to *terrifying* in the span of seconds was sometimes disconcerting.

"I don't wanna go back—"

"Penny," Naz murmured, his hand cutting between them like he was drawing an invisible line there, "it's not happening. It's *not*."

Right, right.

So, why didn't her brain hear that, too?

Then, to the principal, Naz lost his friendly, willing-to-please facade when he said, "She's not moving out of this school. I've already paid for her year—her graduation isn't that far away. Her grades are passable. She's kept up with online classes and the minimum classwork needed to stay above board. And what, because she won't engage with people the way *you* think is acceptable, you're willing to push her out altogether? Give me a fucking break."

"Excuse me, just who do you think—"

"You know exactly who I am," Naz muttered, standing from his chair and stretching to his full height. Penny quickly moved to follow. "What do you want—more money? I heard they're looking to add to the gym facilities and upgrade current equipment. Send me a memo. A check will follow. In the meantime, make a little more space for Penny while she finishes her year here and *without* bullshit like this that wastes my time. She's already been victimized enough outside of these walls. Let's not add to it while we get her to graduation day."

The principal gaped, silent.

Naz smiled again. "Anything else?"

"I …"

"I'll take that as a no. Penny, let's go."

"Okay," she whispered, quickly scrambling around the chairs to follow after Naz. On their way out of the office, Naz snatched the phone from Penny's hand without regard to her question of, "What are you doing?"

He plugged in a number, then handed it back saying, "If they give you any shit here after today, and you need somebody to get here fast, but Roz and I aren't available, call Luca. That's his number. He'll drop everything and be here, okay?"

Penny quieted, glancing down at the new contact staring back at her. Naz didn't miss it.

"You seemed okay with him—sorry, I didn't mean to assume. Are you not?"

The empty corridor of the school leading away from the office echoed with their footsteps. She had to ask herself that same question while a warmth bloomed in her chest at the idea of having Luca available to her with nothing more than a phone call. It was almost enough to make her smile.

And that was *crazy*.

Dumb, even.

It certainly didn't help that the guy made her tongue-tied just by being near, and that she didn't even know why. Was she *okay* with it?

Confused more than anything.

Eventually, Penny muttered, "Yeah, it's okay."

Sort of.

"And thank you," she added.

Naz frowned. "For what?"

"That. Back there with Tippens."

He stopped walking. Penny turned to face Naz at the same time.

"I guess," she said when he continued staring at her while saying nothing, "I'm still surprised you guys keep doing anything for me at all when I don't do very much for you except … *be* here. In the way."

"You're not in the way, for one. And don't be surprised about shit. This is what we do for people we love, Penny. We take care of them. We take care of *you*." He didn't give her time to consider his words before he said,

"Therapist appointment next, right?"

Penny nodded, her throat thick with an emotion she hadn't expected. "Yeah."

• • •

Therapy was the same as it always was which meant Penny zoned out the second she sat on the chair facing the windows. For a while, Dr. Tangler was willing to play along with her patient's typical behavior, but then she asked a question that couldn't be ignored.

"Are you willing to talk about your father today?" the therapist asked.

Penny snapped out of her haze in an instant. "Talk about what, specifically?"

"Well—"

"I did hours of victim testimony. Sat in front of cameras while I talked to detective after detective. And I know you were given access to all of it, so what exactly do you want me to say to you about him that I haven't already said?"

Over her shoulder, she found the therapist staring back at her instead of down at the pad in her hands that she constantly scribbled notes throughout their sessions. What Penny would give to get a single peek at those notes even once.

What did the woman write about her?

What did she *think*?

Probably nothing worse than what Penny dealt with on her own. It couldn't be.

"For those things," Dr. Tangler replied, "you detailed the sexual abuse and circumstances of your situation over the years. I was thinking—"

"It's all the *same*. Him. What he did to me. Nothing is different now."

"How about his death, for starters. We could talk about that and if that's had any—"

"He got what he deserved," Penny said, a venom coating every single word. And she didn't regret it, even when the doctor's eyes widened at her patient's outburst. "And he's where he belongs, too."

In hell.

She hoped he burnt there forever.

Turning back to the window, Penny ignored the sound of a pen scratching against paper behind her. She expected the woman to push the topic a little more—as if every other time Preston Dunsworth was brought into their sessions, and she refused to talk about it would change.

Instead, the therapist changed the subject. Entirely.

"How are things at home with Nazio and Rosalynn?"

Penny's brow dipped. "Fine. Why?"

"I wonder if you're happy there or if … things have changed at all. I wanted to ask if you noticed anything that made you uncomfortable or that you might want to chat about with me while you're here."

That didn't sit right.

Penny didn't know why.

*Red flag number one.*

This was the first time the therapist ever asked about Naz and Roz in such a way. If anything, the doctor seemed to like the way Penny responded to her guardians and being in their custody. It wasn't an issue.

Why was she searching for one?

"Has anything concerned you—maybe business within the home—with them?" the doctor asked. "Anything at all?"

Penny turned on the chair, making it spin on the pedestal to face the therapist. "What do you mean?"

"Anything. Maybe they … argue. Or perhaps you've noticed things aren't always as they seem as they come and go. Have you noticed any criminal activity—"

"What?"

Penny wasn't stupid. Like every other teenage girl in America, she also had access to the internet. She knew who Naz and Roz were, where they came from … their family's legacy in the criminal underworld. The few exchanges she had—mostly with Naz—about the undercurrent of the mafia side of things made it clear she shouldn't concern herself with something that didn't involve her.

They weren't above board. But they also weren't bad people. Not the kind of people who hurt her, anyway. Penny was very black and white in that way. Things either were or they were not.

"I'm asking," the therapist said when Penny remained mute in the chair, "because your caseworker is concerned that your current residence might not be the best place for you considering some of the recent actions and notes from your school. She wanted me to bring up these issues with you and see how you felt."

"You mean, how *you* feel," Penny returned. "Because that's what it boils down to here, right? What *you* think and feel about me. It goes into your little notes there—" she waved at the notepad in the doctor's hands "—and then you pass it on to the caseworker who I barely even see and can't remember her name. And then she comes around occasionally, to tell people who take care of me what they're doing wrong all because she read some bullshit written on paper. Right?"

She had a scary realization, then.

One that took her breath away and hurt worse than even the memories that chased her daily. These doctors and her caseworker, they could take her away from the only people who ever cared. People who *helped* her …

who protected her without asking for anything in return.

People who loved her.

People *she* loved.

Because she did.

*Love them.*

"Penny—"

"If they try to take me away from Naz and Roz," she told the therapist, "it'll be the last thing the state ever does to me."

She had another thirty minutes on the clock with Dr. Tangler, but it didn't make a single difference to what she did next. Standing from the chair, Penny snatched the coat hanging off the arm and headed out of the office even as the therapist called out behind her. She didn't stop walking until she was outside and sitting in the passenger seat of Naz's new Roadster.

He looked her way, brow raised when he said, "That was too fast. What happened?"

Penny pressed a hand against her heart, willing the organ to slow down and stop hurting. "She asked questions … about you, and Roz."

'What kind of—"

"Nothing *good*."

Naz dragged in a sharp breath. "You mean like … business? The *family*?"

Penny only shrugged, muttering, "Said the caseworker brought it up and suggested she mention it to me. Like they want to look into the home and if it's the right place for me or not. Are they going to remove me from—"

"No."

"But—"

Naz reached over and grabbed Penny's hand with his own. It was the first and only time the man had touched her, but instead of pulling away like she would for anyone else, there was stability in the action.

*Comfort.*

"Penny, you're not going anywhere unless you want to," he said. "Do you hear me?"

Water had welled in her eyes, making everything a bit blurry. Still, she met his dark gaze as she asked, "Promise?"

"Absolutely."

"Okay."

But even through the tears that she was trying to hold back, Penny could see Naz wasn't happy. She knew it wasn't because of her, but that didn't make the situation any better.

"It's going to be okay, right?" she asked.

"You focus on *you* … whatever you need, getting better, just focus on you." Naz shrugged, adding, "That's all Roz and I ever wanted you to do. We'll handle the rest."

But how?
She decided it was better not to ask.

# *INTERLUDE: 1.*

*Present Day …*

"HEY, Penny."

Whether it was the shock of someone saying her name, or just the fact that they had managed to sneak up on her in the forest behind Naz and Roz's property, it still earned a reaction from Penny. She hadn't heard the approach from her left until the new voice joined a silent conversation she'd been having inside her head while the memories raced for attention in her mind.

Despite her years of training to stand calm and steady no matter the situation, she let out a yelp and fell backward when she stumbled over an exposed root of a tree. The white strands of her hair made a curtain over her eyes as her palms hit the ground to catch her fall from turning into something much worse.

A quiet, child-like laugh rang out in the forest. The sound was almost musical and a total contrast to the way her heart thumped loudly in her chest.

"Sorry," her new companion said, "I didn't mean to scare you."

Penny didn't bother to get up, or even fix her hair. Instead, she pushed sideways and came to sit right on her ass, so she could stare directly at the guest who had joined her in the forest. He was maybe three and half feet tall, not quite four, *if that.* Dark hair. *Soul-deep eyes.* She found familiarity in the softness of his boyish features. Even the way his grin tilted a little more on the right side was a smirk she had seen time and time again.

She didn't need to ask his name.

She already knew.

"Cross," she said.

The boy shrugged. "Well, everybody calls me *little* Cross when they think I can't hear. I don't like that very much. But since Grandpapa doesn't like being called Senior, I have to deal with it. Or that's what he said."

His words were clear. His sentences, smart. For his age, anyway.

"And you are, right—*Penny*, I mean?"

She stared at the boy, blinking as if he might disappear in the next minute. She was still trying to figure out why in the hell he was even in the woods. Where were his parents? Was this something he did on the regular?

*Hell …*

Penny hadn't seen his face since he was six months old. Not once in all the years since she left had she even been graced with a picture of the boy as he grew. She always wondered, of course … did he keep his father's features, or change to look more like his mom?

She missed a lot.

About him.

His first steps.

Those first words.

Even his first day at school.

"You don't talk?" Cross asked. "Ma says you were always quiet."

She swallowed hard, knowing what she *needed* to tell the boy because she wasn't even supposed to be here in the first place. "I don't know who you think I am, but I'm not—"

"Yeah, you're Penny. I have pictures."

So sure.

And *true*.

God.

Penny dragged in a quick breath. "You didn't scare m—"

"Yeah, I did," he interjected again, seemingly unbothered that he kept interrupting her. "Sorry. It *was* kind of funny, though."

She couldn't help the smile fighting to get out. He was quite the kid. It only killed her more.

"You know they're looking for you, right?" Cross asked.

Penny wet her lips. "How do *you* know that?"

"Uncle Luca came back. I heard Papa say he was lying. There was *a lot* of yelling."

"You call him your uncle?"

Cross lifted one shoulder covered by a leather jacket that looked *strikingly* like one his father would have worn years ago. The children's Doc Martens on his feet matched the whole vibe. The one thing he didn't have was the slicked-back hair, but the wild strands of his black hair looked better all crazy anyway.

"He's my godfather, too," Luca added. "So …"

Penny knew.

"And you're supposed to be my godmother."

"Yeah, I am," she admitted quietly.

"*Supposed to be*," the boy said again, "because you're not here. You never were. And even though everybody else knows you, I don't."

"You knew me. Just for a short time."

That didn't satisfy the boy at all.

"Yeah, well. Not the same." He sighed hard, glancing through the trees at his house when he said, "I like it out here. I'm not supposed to go past the trees, but … well, I do what I want."

Penny laughed under her breath. "We all do."

"Not like me."

What did that mean?

"You're smart, aren't you?" she asked.

Cross pressed his lips together as he considered that before saying, "Yeah, but not like my papa. Different."

"How?"

"He's … smart-*smart*, you know? Numbers, and books, and *things*. All the things. Universe stuff. I see people and just *know*."

Penny's brow dipped. "Know what?"

Cross looked back her way, those soul-deep brown eyes of his piercing and *apprehensive* and knowing when he replied, "Well, everything, Penny."

She thought … *no way*.

"Really?"

The boy smiled half-heartedly, saying, "It's a lot sometimes. People lie, I know. When people hurt, I see it. Ma says it makes me special. Papa says … it is what it is."

"And what do you think?"

"I think you ask about me because you don't want me to ask about *you*."

And just like that, Penny knew he was telling her the truth.

"I should go," Penny said, pushing up from the ground and brushing the dirt from her backside at the same time.

Cross glanced her way, frowning openly. "Remember when I said I didn't know you?"

"Yeah."

"I did know enough *about* you. I know you must have loved me before you left and made my ma and papa sad, right? Because you made me something to keep—something I would always have." Cross shuffled his feet against the dry ground, kicking up some dirt and dead leaves in the process when he muttered, "I mean, nobody makes a song for someone else just *because*."

Some did.

Not Penny.

"Of course, I loved you."

Dark eyes of a five-and-a-half-year-old lifted to meet hers when he asked, "Then why did you leave?"

# 7.

*Luca*

SMOKE curled upward from the burning cigarette dangling between Luca's fingers. He was more interested in finishing his cigarette than fucking with the men currently moving back and forth between the pile of boxes in the alley and the shipping truck where they loaded the packages of illegal cigarettes. In a couple of days, the truckload of cigarettes would make their way across the Canadian border to sell for twenty-five bucks a pop.

A whole truck was easy money.

Besides, he wasn't there to *do* the work with the crew of guys. Just overlook their work. He could do that perfectly fine from where he sat on the tailgate.

He wished that was all he was doing, but the voice in his ear—his father talking to him through the Bluetooth while Luca kept an eye on the guys—kept him somewhat engaged. At least today, Zeke wasn't being a total fucking asshole.

Things were looking up.

*Right?*

"Good to know you're keeping busy watching Naz's guys," his father said. "I'm sure he appreciates the help, too."

"He's … got other things to handle."

Not that Luca needed to mention what those things were exactly. Everyone in their circles knew that Naz was still trying to get his house and life settled a little more. Months after Penny moved in and changed everything, and some days weren't any better than when she first arrived honestly.

His friend didn't give up, though.

Luca respected that.

"Either way," Zeke murmured on the call. "I'm proud of you."

*Happy*, he thought his father meant to say. Zeke was happy his son was doing what he thought he should have been doing from the moment he graduated high school—handling family business.

Luca didn't call his father out on the distinction, but he also didn't have to.

"Despite what you may think," Zeke continued, "because I do know how you think, for the record. I was you once."

"Were you, now?"

"Well, not exactly the same. But enough."

*Hmm.*

"And," his father added like the man hadn't already said enough for Luca to think about you, "I'm only hard on you because no one else is. Something to consider, yeah?"

Was it?

He might have questioned his father a little more on the topic, but the familiar man that rounded the rear of the shipping truck stopped him from saying anything other than, "Gotta get back to work, Dad."

"All right. Call your mother later—she misses you."

"Will do."

*Maybe.*

If he had the time.

It seemed like Luca didn't have a lot of that lately, but he wouldn't apologize for his lack of presence because of it, either. He couldn't be all the things, all the time. Some shit had to give whether everyone liked it, or not.

He ended the call with his father and stuffed the phone into the pocket of his leather jacket just in time to greet Naz as the man came to stand in front of Luca.

"Working hard or hardly working?" Naz asked, grinning.

Luca pulled the last drag from the cigarette before tossing the butt to the ground without care. The sparks bounced over the asphalt like small fireworks as he smirked back at his friend. "Since when do I have to actually *do* the work?"

Naz laughed. "Fair point. They keeping straight?"

"Doing fine, man. They don't give me shit. No trouble."

"Good. That's what I wanna hear."

Even as Naz said that, his gaze followed the group of three guys that came back to the rear of the truck with another armload of boxes. None of the young men—ranging in age from seventeen to twenty-three—passed a second look at the arrival of their actual boss. The boys were accustomed to Naz coming and going at times. If anything, it should prove to the guys that their boss trusted them enough to do what he told them to do, and without issue, when he was comfortable leaving them to work with someone else to oversee their business.

A guy needed a good crew to do that.

Not every Capo had one.

"Nice chunk of change in there," Luca said, referring to the cartons of illegal cigarettes.

Naz shrugged. "Exactly, *change*. But shit, it keeps them well paid for the month, and I can't complain about that. It's a little job in the grand scheme, but the boys gotta eat, too."

*Right.*

"And," Naz added, his dark gaze coming to settle on his friend sitting on the tailgate, "was that your father I heard you talking to?"

Luca rolled his eyes, pushing off the back of the tailgate to stand at his full height. Next to Naz, the two were about eye level give or take an inch. As kids, he was always shorter than his best friend, and it only added to the whole *following along* complex that developed over the years for him. Now, it wasn't so bad. Not that it had ever been a thing for Nazio.

"He's happy. I'm doing work for you. What can he bitch about?"

Naz sighed. "Who else is gonna give us trouble, huh?"

He gave Naz a second look.

His friend only shrugged.

Zeke had said something similar, but Luca still didn't like it. Nor did he think it was particularly right, either. Who was he to say, though?

He didn't have a kid.

Might never.

Who knew?

Stuffing his hands in the pocket of the hoodie he'd thrown on under the leather jacket, he waited until the guys came back out of the truck and headed for another armload of boxes before saying more to Naz.

"Since when do you show up while I'm looking after the guys, anyway?" Luca asked. "Checking up on me, or—"

Naz chuckled, shaking his head. "Don't even start. You know I don't worry about you or what you're doing."

"Had to ask."

"Well, don't."

"Something is wrong, then," Luca noted. All it took was his friend's lifting brow to know he had hit the nail right on the head with that assumption. "What happened?"

"Bullshit, that's what."

Luca chuffed under his breath. "That tells me everything."

"I'm getting around to it."

"Well, get there *faster*."

Naz only rolled his eyes at Luca's attitude, but that was just their way. Another made man, and he wouldn't dare talk to the guy the way he did with his friend. But that was the thing … Naz would always be his best friend first and everything else second. He didn't know how to switch that shit off, and really, he didn't want to.

Maybe that was his biggest problem with the family business. He didn't know how to separate the lines that were so clearly drawn the way other men wanted and needed him to on a regular basis. Men like his father.

Oh, well.

It was what it was.

"Anyway," Naz muttered, shifting from foot to foot while the guys came back around for another trip inside the truck, "I've got a new problem that needs to be handled as soon as possible, so it doesn't grow into something more."

"And that problem is …?"

Naz shot him a look. "Penny's caseworker. Apparently, the woman decided she should step in on Penny's therapy sessions by suggesting to the therapist that our home might not be the right place for her. So much so, that she even encouraged the woman to ask about things going on *inside* or out of the home. Like business. Or rather, anything out of the ordinary. *Criminal activity* was actually said, apparently."

That had Luca's brow rising. "Really?"

"Yeah."

"That's … bold."

"And complete fucking bullshit," Naz grumbled.

"You know, considering who you are and everything, you guys were lucky to even get guardianship over Penny in the first damn place," Luca said, wetting his lips to remove what taste remained of the nicotine. "And don't pretend like you didn't have to pull some strings just to make that happen, either. I know better."

Naz lifted one shoulder, unbothered. "And?"

"I'm just saying. Probably should have expected some shit like this might pop up over time. People like us can only get away with so much before it becomes too much, you know what I mean?"

"I don't need it pointed out."

"Fair enough. What do you plan to do about this problem? Or … what do you want me to do about it? Because that's why you're here, right? You want me to do something."

Naz didn't even try to hide his smile. "You're not wrong … we don't need this problem with the caseworker right now on top of everything else."

"So, what do you need me to do?"

"Get a leg up on the problem. Get us ahead of it before it turns into something bigger than it already is, and we have to handle that accordingly. I would rather not get to that point, you know? The woman—Penny's caseworker—is just misguided. She doesn't know us … that's fine, she doesn't need to. She does need to back off, though. Find something to make that happen for me."

Luca could do that.

He could find anything.

The only thing he needed to know was … "Who is the caseworker?"

He could do the rest.

# *8.*

## *Penny*

BY the time Friday rolled around the following week, things had gone well. Or, better than Penny expected, anyway. That said something. Maybe getting her guardian called into the school for a sit-down with the principal wasn't such a bad thing.

Her teachers laid off. She *did* make an effort to complete assignments even if a few were a little late. No one complained. As for the other stuff the principal mentioned … well, she still wasn't going to pretend like she cared about making friends with the other students or joining in on activities where she had a choice in the matter.

Win some, lose some.

That was life, right?

Besides, the school was the last thing on Penny's mind as a more important date approached. Roz's baby shower, that was. It had been on the back of her mind for weeks, and she still hadn't figured out what to get Roz for the baby …

Was it silly?

Maybe.

Roz wouldn't care what Penny bought her for a gift, really. Even she knew that. Still, she wanted to do something … if not for Roz, then for the baby boy that would soon be someone else in her life to love. Because she did—love him—already, and he wasn't even born yet. Maybe she cared so much about the baby because Roz had kept Penny informed and included with the pregnancy from almost the second she moved in with her new guardians.

It gave her something to look forward to … a reason to stick around, even. Not that she ever told Roz that fact. Every doctor's appointment and ultrasound brought them closer to the day when the baby became *real.* If that made any sense at all.

Just buying any old thing off the shelf didn't seem good enough. Not for Penny, anyway. She wanted to do more.

It only seemed fair.

Speaking of the baby …

While her locker was open and she was changing out her books for one class to what she needed for the next, Penny took a moment to check Roz's last text. It was a picture of her latest ultrasound. A 3D image, this time.

Penny would have gone along to see the baby on the screen in flesh-tone colors with his little face so clear to greet them, but … she *was* trying to do better with the whole attendance thing.

Somewhat.

If she wasn't doing it for herself—because she really didn't give a shit about this place or the diploma everyone kept saying she needed—then she was trying to do it for Roz and Naz. Hadn't she already caused them enough shit with the caseworker? No need to give that woman another reason to make a fuss.

Did they want her at school?

*Fine.*

She was here.

What she did here … well, that was another matter.

She took a second to enlarge the picture in the text thread, enjoying the sight of the baby's ultrasound image even if he did look like a funny little demon with oddly shaped skin and red circles where his eyes should be. Roz had warned her that the 3D imaging might be … funky. But it did give them a better idea of how the baby would look when he was born.

And it did.

Penny texted back, *He looks like Naz.*

Because he did.

Baby Cross—Roz did settle on that for a name—had the same shaped nose and face as his father. The dark hair on top of his head was clearly visible. She bet when he was born and finally opened his eyes to say hello to the world, they would be the same dark brown-black as his dad's, too.

*I said that, too*, Roz replied fast. *And he was sucking his thumb. I'll show you those pictures later. How's classes today?*

*Boring*, Penny thought. Which was absolutely nothing new. Teachers who encouraged her to join her classmates in group work that she had no plans on doing. Classes that made her want to sleep, but the credits were required to graduate. *And* she had gym after her next class which was always a special kind of hell because she refused to wear the same shorts and t-shirt that everyone else did.

Like these asshole teenagers needed another reason to stare at Penny and whisper behind her back. They did that enough without her showing off all her scars and giving them even more reasons to be a bunch of pricks.

Instead of saying the truth, she simply wrote back, *Fine.* Roz didn't need to worry. Not today. She was handling baby stuff, and that's all she should be thinking about. Certainly not *Penny.*

Was that growth?

To know … people had lives that didn't—or shouldn't, rather—revolve around constantly making sure Penny was doing what she should be when she was more than capable?

She wasn't sure.

Did it even matter?

The ringing bell overhead took Penny's attention away from the screen of her phone just long enough for her to roll her eyes. *Great.* Now she was going to be late to her next class because it was in the next wing over.

Oh, well.

She texted a quick goodbye to Roz, grabbed the last book she needed from her locker, and then stepped back to slam the metal door shut. She was just reaching for the lock to close it when she noticed the guy who had come to lean against the row of lockers. Maybe, had she not been so distracted with her conversation, then she might have noticed him slipping in beside her and could have done something before he surprised her.

Penny hated that.

Specifically, right beside *hers.*

Caleb was his name.

Caleb Knight.

A stupid, rich, popular fuck that messed with the same girls who made it their first and only job to piss Penny off every chance they could for a straight month after she started attending the private high school. With a spot on the baseball team, the guy earned his ranking in the upper  of who was who in the school.

Except she didn't care.

"Hey, Penny," Caleb said, grinning. "You busy?"

She arched a brow, not bothering with his attempt at small talk. Because *why*? It was a waste of her time and his. There was only one reason why this guy approached her, and it was not because he wanted to make friends. The group of kids watching them from twenty feet down the hall like they were waiting for the circus to start said she wasn't wrong in her assumption, either.

"What do you want?" she asked, locking the locker. "I have a class to get to."

"We can't talk? You've been here like—"

"*What do you want?*"

Caleb stuck a hand in his pocket as he turned to lean his shoulder against the lockers instead of his back like before. Now, he was facing her and that grin of his felt … *untrue.* Sinister, even. It bothered her that she recognized those expressions in other people before they even proved themselves to be out for their own agenda.

Life taught her how.

"Don't be a bitch," he said. "I'm just trying to talk."

"Right," Penny scoffed, grabbing her book bag from the floor. "Well, I'm not in the mood to *talk.* So, see you lat—"

"Wait a sec."

Penny turned to ice as everything moved in slow motion around her when Caleb reached over to grab the tail end of her braided hair. Flipped over her shoulder, the white braid was more than she usually did with her hair when even running a brush through it some mornings felt like a chore. She was getting better about that, too—taking care of *herself*.

Someone *touching* her, though?

A chill froze her to the spot.

"It's *Dunsworth*, right?" Caleb asked, twisting the strands of her hair between the pads of his fingers. Penny couldn't *move*. Why was he touching her? Why did people think they could just touch someone without even asking? "Preston—that was your dad. Preston Dunsworth."

All at once, Penny snapped out of her fear. All she needed was hearing her father's name on this stupid fuck's mouth to do it.

She jerked away from Caleb, her book bag tight in her grasp. Out of his reach, she at least felt a little safer and was able to *talk*. Or rather, tell this guy to go fuck himself with a sharp object.

"Get the fuck away from me," Penny snapped.

"So, that's a yes?" He winked. "If that's true … is it also true what he used to do? Did he really pimp you out to anyone who could afford the price? Is that still available, or …?"

His gaze trailed up and down Penny's form. She was forced to wear the same stupid uniform as every other girl in the school except she opted for the slacks the boys wore and usually kept an oversized, zip-up hoodie on hand to throw over the button-down and tie that was made mandatory by the dress code. Today was no exception.

It didn't stop Caleb from looking.

Nothing did with *creeps*.

They were all the same.

Then, Caleb dared to step forward.

Closer to her.

*Again*.

Penny wasn't going to let him touch her—once was enough and even then, that was too much. Before he could even try, she reared back and threw a fist that landed against Caleb's smirking mouth. She felt the way his teeth smooshed against her knuckles, leaving an ache behind when her hand fell back at her side.

He hit the lockers.

Laughter roared from down the hall.

Penny was already leaving, spinning on her heels and heading in the opposite direction from the students *and* her next class. Someone called her name when she turned the corner at the end of the hall, but she didn't care to look for who.

Fuck all of them.

She didn't bother to call Roz.

Or Naz.

They were both busy—baby stuff. Not that they needed to worry about a silly thing like her punching someone in the mouth. The school would probably fill in those details. Why did she have to?

Instead, she texted Luca. She might as well put that *drop everything* promise Naz made to the test.

Right?

# *9.*

*Luca*

*I need help.*

Three words. That was all Luca needed to drop everything he was doing for Naz—the little issue of a caseworker sticking her nose where it didn't belong—and head a few blocks away. At least, Penny didn't make him search for her. Her second text added, *Don't rush. I'm at the gas station a block away from the school.*

Well, too late.

He did rush.

Shit, it was the first time the girl even used his number since Naz had given it to her. Luca wasn't about to make her wait when she had to use it in the first place. He figured she probably hadn't bothered to call Naz or Roz because they were busy with appointments in the heart of the city. Not that it would have mattered as, like him, they would have dropped everything to run for Penny, too.

He didn't mind doing it, though.

By the time Luca pulled his car into the gas station, Penny had made herself a seat on the bench that faced the pumps. With her hoodie pulled over her head, she sat cross-legged on the seat with an open bag of chips in her lap.

*Hey.*

She wasn't in a state. No tears, by the looks of it. From what he could see through the windshield, there were no visible marks on her to say someone was going to have to die. He counted those as all good things.

The rest was yet to be determined.

All it took was one beat of the car's horn, and Penny pushed away from the bench. She dropped the bag of chips into a garbage bin as she passed it by before coming to the passenger side of his car. Opening the door, she tossed her book bag to the floor of the car and stepped in second, falling into the seat like it was the only thing she was waiting for.

A safe place.

He didn't take the car out of park or move a muscle to suggest they were going to leave as fast as he arrived. He glanced at her from the side when he asked, "You okay?"

Sky blue stared back at him. Maybe she hadn't been crying when he arrived, but the bloodshot eyes said she did cry at some point. The twisting tug in his chest hurt at the very idea. Didn't people realize this girl had been hurt enough?

Why add insult to the injury?

Penny only shrugged under the baggy, zip-up black hoodie. A bit of her braid hung out from the hood, the white strands of hair a bright contrast against the dark fabric. "I am now."

"But you weren't."

"It's not a big deal."

He didn't believe that for a second.

Apparently, neither did Penny.

"Okay, that's a lie," she muttered, looking away from his unmoveable stare. "It *was* a big deal, but I don't want to let it be. The more people know shit bothers me; the more they'll use it to do exactly that, too. People can do what they want or say whatever but only I get to decide if it hurts me. You know?"

He did, but … "Just tell me what happened. If anything, so I can decide whether it's something we need to handle right now or wait until later."

Penny rolled her eyes. "That's so …"

"Yeah?"

"Responsible."

Luca barked out a laugh. "Yeah, nobody said this growing up shit was any fun."

He learned that a long time ago.

She only sighed.

He let her have a moment.

Eventually, Penny turned back to him but then, her eyes were lined with unshed tears. It made her already wide, bright eyes look even *bigger*. Impossibly so. Like one of those white-skinned China dolls that people kept safe on high shelves away from hands that might play a little too rough. Too many people had done exactly that to this girl, too. Treated her like a doll and then played with her like one as if she wasn't a real person with a heart and soul of her own.

"A guy—Caleb—said some stuff about my father. And me," Penny added lower. "About … things. I don't want to say what. Doesn't matter anyway. Kind of obvious."

"You don't have to say anything."

She said enough, frankly.

Teenagers were terrible. Teenage *boys* were little bastards on their good days. Luca could say that because he had been one of them once. He had never been purposefully awful to other people—or females, for that matter—but that wasn't always the case. Things happened. It wasn't an excuse for shitty behavior—he also couldn't say he was surprised, either.

"I think he only did it to be funny for his friends," Penny said, wiping away the tears that dared to escape with her next blink. As quick as the wet streak graced her pale skin, it was gone like it hadn't existed in the first place. "Because *ha, ha*, it's so fucking funny to be a sex toy for grown men. Asshole."

Luca flinched. "I'm sorry."

"Should have expected it, right? Eventually, *someone* was going to put things together or figure out who I am. It was all over the news. Not like I could pretend—"

"Some people are just cruel because they can be. They don't really understand the weight of the things they say; they just say it for stupid reasons. Fuck him."

That earned him a small smile.

It was something.

"I punched him. There might have been some blood. I don't know, I left pretty fast. I should have stayed right there and done it again."

His first thought?

Good for her.

His second?

*Yikes.*

That wasn't going to help the caseworker thing, never mind the fact that the school already had a hard nut for Penny, according to Naz. Luca decided that then probably wasn't the time to point any of that out.

Then, he murmured, "I should call Naz and Roz, though. At least, let them know something happened so they have a heads-up before the school calls to inform them. Better they hear it from me—or *you*."

Penny frowned. "Yeah, okay. Will you do it?"

"Sure."

Why the hell not?

He thought it was better for her to be the one who delivered the news, but why argue? The day had undoubtedly been traumatic enough for Penny without him adding to it by forcing her to do something else she wasn't comfortable with.

Naz's phone rang twice before he picked up Luca's call. The first thing out of his friend's mouth was, "Is she okay?"

Luca passed a look Penny's way, saying, "He knows."

Her face scrunched up.

*Well …*

Some shit couldn't be helped.

"She's fine," he told Naz. "Called me right away and I made the trip over to pick her up. As far as that goes, I've got it under control. The school, though … that's another matter."

"Fuck them."

Luca chuckled. "Yeah, I know, man."

"We're on our way home, so—"

"I'll bring her your way, then."

"No," Penny said suddenly, bringing Luca's attention back to her for a second. She shrugged, picking at her nails and avoiding his stare when she whispered, "I just … I don't want to go home right now. Can we do something? Drive or—"

"Change of plans," Luca told his friend, not even bothering to decide *what* he was going to do with Penny. Something. He had an idea. "I'll bring her home a little later, okay?"

"You sure?" Naz asked.

"Yeah, man. No worries."

He could handle a seventeen-year-old.

Right?

"Call me if anything changes," Naz said.

"Will do."

Discarding the phone to the cup holder after he ended the call, Luca tipped his head Penny's way, asking her, "Anything you want to do or is it up to me?"

"Well, what did you want to do?"

He stared at the girl, taking her in and realizing … his mother had been right. Penny was a young woman struggling between what once was and what would be. She was at a strange time in her life, too, a place between childhood and growing into an adult where nothing would be the same as it used to be. And all of that was *on top* of the shit she already had to deal with. While some of it merged, because that was inevitable, not all of it did. They were separate issues.

Did she even realize that?

"Do you talk to anybody?" he asked.

Penny's brow dipped. "Like my therapist?"

"More like … someone who *knows*, Penny. Somebody that gets you and what's happened. Do you have *anybody* like that? A friend, even."

"Not really."

Good to know.

Luca planned on fixing that.

Putting the car in drive, he shot Penny a smile when he said, "We're gonna go see my mom. I think you should spend some time with her."

"I … have?"

Luca scoffed. "Nah, not like you should. I mean, without other people around. Not sitting down for a family dinner when everyone is on their best behavior. No, you need to *really* meet my mom and spend some time with her. Just you and her. She's kind of amazing."

"You said … someone who knows. Does she? *Know*, I mean?"

His smile drifted away, then. "Unfortunately, she knows what you're dealing with better than most. Nobody should know these kinds of things—if the world was perfect, no one would. But she does."

"Oh."

*Yeah.*

What else needed to be said?

• • •

"Should I just stay in the car until—"

"No," Luca said, laughing under his breath as he pushed open the driver's door. "Family is welcome at this house anytime. All you need to do is show up and walk through the front door."

"But I'm not …" Penny's words trailed off when Luca glanced over his shoulder at her. Maybe it was the way he raised his eyebrow that quieted her, but either way, he saw the acceptance flash in her eyes when she muttered, "Okay, I'm coming."

*Good.*

Penny stayed behind Luca as he climbed the front steps to his childhood home. He didn't bother to knock on the door before he opened it up and headed inside. As Penny kicked off her shoes, and he did the same, he yelled down the quiet hall.

"Ma?"

He expected his mother to pop out of the kitchen where she liked to spend most of her afternoon cooking and prepping for dinner. Despite the fact she no longer had a whole house to feed, his mother still managed to cook for a small army every single day. If he ever wanted leftovers, the only thing he needed to do was show up.

And he tried.

*Often.*

Or as much as he could lately.

"Luca?"

Sure enough, his mother appeared in the doorway of the kitchen with a dishtowel in her hands. Her confusion quickly melted away at the sight of him and Penny waiting down the hall. He didn't get to see his mother enough and even he knew it. So, when he did randomly show up like this, the last thing Katya cared about were the details as to why.

Instead of asking what was going on or anything, for that matter, his mother smiled and said, "I'm just making stew and bread. Do you two want anything else?"

Luca laughed. "Nah, Ma. We're good. I just, uh—"

He jerked a thumb back at Penny.

Katya's smile didn't fade even as she raised her brow like she was encouraging him to continue. "Yes?"

"I brought Penny over to say hi. And talk, maybe."

"Talk about what?"

Behind him, Penny shifted from foot to foot, her socks making noise as they rubbed against the entry hallway. "Hi, Mrs. Puzz—"

"Katya," his mother spoke up quickly. "Just call me Katya. Is everything okay? You look … sad."

"It's been a day," Penny muttered.

For a second, his mother said nothing as she looked Luca's way again. He only shrugged in response, hoping that would be enough for Katya to get the hint without him actually needing to give her details. If this entire day ended with Penny talking to his mother about *anything* … then he figured that was a giant leap forward.

Katya was always great at reading the room. Once, she told him because she had to be … a long time ago, knowing the mood of a room before she walked into it was one of the only things that saved her life.

*Yeah.*

His ma really *was* amazing.

Penny could use someone like that in her life. Even if it was just to have someone to talk to that understood what it was like to be *her* … especially in a world that didn't understand at all.

"A rough day?" Katya asked.

"Really rough," Penny muttered.

Katya nodded. "Yeah, that happens. Come on, I'll show you how I braid and cut my bread, so it looks pretty when I put it on the table." Then, to him, his mother said, "And you … your father left some boxes at the basement door that need to go into storage downstairs. Would you do that, so he doesn't have to when he gets home?"

*Nice. Get me out of the way, Ma.*

Luca didn't even mind. "Sure, I'll do it now."

"Thanks. Come with me, Penny."

He shot Penny a wink when she headed past him after his mother who had already disappeared back inside the kitchen. She smiled back. No blush that time, either.

Luca figured maybe he was doing this thing—whatever it was—with Penny right. Except he didn't really know, and it wasn't over yet.

# *10.*

## *Penny*

EVENTUALLY, braiding bread turned into making tea while the stew did its thing in the large pot on the stove. *The longer it stays on the heat, the better it is*, Katya told her as they took their tea upstairs to drink. Penny didn't know if that was true. Cooking wasn't her thing when she was barely able to boil water without forgetting it on the burner. She had to admit there was something wonderful about the smell of freshly cooked bread wafting through the home, though.

And it had been … *calming*.

The very act of kneading the bread to perfection, and then twisting braided strips before cutting precise slices in all the right spots was soothing in a way she hadn't expected. It also kept her talking. Maybe too much, even. She hadn't realized how much easier it would be to share her truth—and *pain*—with someone who had similar experiences.

Katya never told her to stop.

So, she didn't.

Her therapist had suggested group therapy once. A meeting that she could attend once a week in place of one of the days she had to visit the doctor. Women of all ages, as long as they were seventeen or older, came to share stories of their sexual abuse in a therapeutic setting while finding support with others like them.

Penny said no.

*Fast.*

The very idea of sharing in an open setting had sent her anxiety skyrocketing. But one on one with Katya didn't feel so bad or scary. Or maybe … there was just something about her that Penny trusted. She didn't know what it was, and she didn't care as long as it was real.

Now, sitting in Roz's piano room while the two women drank green tea, Katya admitted, "There was a time when I used this room as a place to escape. It was so much easier to be in here for hours a day listening to Roz play than it was anywhere else. I only had one thing to focus on in here, after all."

Hot tea flooded Penny's tongue while she took in those words and decided how she wanted to respond. "Is it still hard sometimes—wanting to hide away, I mean?"

"I won't lie, sometimes it is."

Penny sighed where she sat cross-legged on the piano bench. Lowering the cup between her legs, she said, "Today, a guy at school brought up my father and what he did to me. And maybe that wouldn't have been so bad except he asked if it was still going on. Like, could he get in on the—"

"I'm sorry."

She shrugged.

Katya wasn't accepting that for a minute. "Don't shrug it off, Penny. Don't dismiss that kind of thing like it's just something you should have expected. That makes your brain think you should also *accept* it. And you shouldn't. Ever."

"I didn't. I punched him in the mouth. That's not very accepting to me."

The woman across from her grinned wide, not even ashamed. "Well, fair point, but still … it hurt. It was triggering to you. And it's perfectly fine to say so. *Loudly*, even. Over and over again until people hear you and understand. Your best advocate is yourself."

Penny quieted.

But only for a moment.

"I'm not sure if I'm trying to advocate or just … survive right now."

"I'm sorry to say but that never really goes away," Katya murmured, her soft smile fading when Penny's stare lifted to meet hers. "Things make it easier … time, and life. Finding the right people who make you want to stay on this earth to be with them. The same people that teach you to see yourself as something more than a body to be used. When you're worth something to someone else, when they *love* you, it's easier to love yourself. Eventually, you begin to do those things on your own because we start to rewire."

That was the first time Penny heard that term used.

"Rewire?

Katya laughed, pointing at her temple. "In *here*. It's not right and it takes time to fix it. To *rewire*, so to speak. You've got to give it the time it needs to work."

"Thanks."

"You're on the right track, Penny. You've found the right people to help. My daughter, Naz … even Luca, they all care about you a great deal. *Let them.* And heal while you're at it."

She would keep it in mind.

Penny wiped away the wetness under her eyes with the sleeve of her hoodie, thankful that Katya didn't even mention noticing the tears. She might have been getting better at this whole … *talking* thing, but she didn't want people to point it out. Some shit was still just *hers*.

Even if that meant dealing with it alone, too.

She could do that.

*Mostly.*

"Thanks again." Penny shrugged in response to Katya's raised brow, adding, "For everything … today, I guess."

"I think you should thank someone else for that, huh? I was just here cooking stew."

Yeah, *Luca.*

Couldn't forget about him.

Even if she tried.

Before the two could say anything more, a phone rang somewhere outside the piano room. Katya shot Penny an apologetic smile before standing from the chair, her tea still firmly in her grip as she said, "Let me grab that—you okay to be by yourself for a bit?"

"Yeah, I'm fine. Maybe I'll take a look around."

Despite joining the Puzzas for dinner on occasion, she wasn't actually familiar with their home. Katya didn't seem bothered by the idea.

"I'll find you when I'm done," the woman replied.

"Okay."

When the phone call lasted more than five minutes, Penny decided to head out of the piano room to see what was down the hall. She passed a bathroom on the way, but it was what she found at the far end of the hallway that interested her the most.

The bedroom looked like it belonged to a typical teenage boy. Right down to the black and gray sheets on the double bed, and the posters of bands and women on the walls. She couldn't help but wonder why Katya and her husband hadn't changed the room or even, done something different with it.

Instead, it kind of seemed like a tribute to their son. Or who he used to be before he grew up, anyway. Despite that, the space still felt welcoming. If that made any sense. She was *comfortable* in the room.

In the corner of the room, three guitars sat in stands looking like they hadn't been played in a while … which was a shame. The desk and chair closer to the door caught Penny's attention and drew her near to look at the framed pictures on the top.

Picking up the first, she couldn't help but smile at the boys who grinned back from the photograph. They hadn't changed that much—not in their looks, anyway. Naz and Luca stood arm in arm, dripping wet in swim shorts with a pool behind them. They had to be, *maybe*, her age or younger in the photo.

*Always friends*, she thought.

She couldn't imagine what that was like—to have one single person who remained something akin to *her* for most of her life. It was a strange concept, but not one that scared her. It just seemed unreal because that had been so far from her reality. Before she was shoved from one private school to the next to get her out of her parents' lives, her social interactions were limited to the people approved by her mother and father.

People who didn't *know*.

Or even … people who wouldn't tell.

Penny shook those thoughts away as she replaced the photo to the desk and grabbed a second. This one was just Luca—dressed in a three-piece suit with a red vest and tie, he didn't look any older in this photo than the other. Maybe it was a prom or a formal dance.

And then she wondered …

What might have happened if she met him under different circumstances? If they were the same age, would things be different—would she know what to do with the silly crush that still kept her heart in a tight grip every time he was within breathing distance?

What would it be like if she wasn't … broken?

"Find something interesting?"

The familiar voice behind Penny damn near made her drop the framed photograph straight to the desk. Somehow, she managed to keep a hold of it and set it down without incident. Not even able to *pretend* like she wasn't embarrassed about being caught in the bedroom, she tried to smile it off.

"Sorry, I was just—"

Katya didn't look bothered when she interjected, "It's fine. We leave the door open. Luca doesn't even use this room when he stays the night … which is basically never now."

Her cheeks were still red.

She could *feel* the heat.

Katya's gaze drifted from the photo Penny had just been looking at to the other one on the desk that had clearly been moved a couple of inches as well. "Do you like my son?"

Penny wasn't sure what she expected the woman to say, but *that* wasn't it. At least, not so brazenly. It certainly didn't help with the blush in her cheeks.

"It doesn't matter," Penny mumbled, stepping away from the desk and heading for the doorway. "He doesn't know I exist. Not like I know he does, anyway. Not like *that*."

He didn't look at Penny and get confused. He didn't see her and think … *God, that's the most beautiful face I've ever seen.* She didn't give him butterflies or silly, stupid thoughts the way he did for her.

And why should he?

Penny was … mousey.

*Small.*

She faded away more than she stood out.

"And he shouldn't know," Penny added, attempting to step past Katya.

The woman didn't move. "You're right … you're a bit too young for him right now."

"And a mess."

Katya tipped her head to the side, eyeing Penny. "But not unworthy. We already talked about that, remember? Being who you are—going through the things you did—none of it makes you unworthy of finding someone to love. Or someone who loves you."

That said, Katya stepped to the side, finally letting Penny pass. As she did so, the older woman added, "And even if something isn't in the cards right now because of circumstance doesn't mean that will always be the case. Everything takes time, Penny. It's just one breath after another until it starts to feel normal. Try to keep it in mind."

She just kept walking.

And *hoping*.

Hoping maybe Katya was right.

Even if that terrified her.

• • •

Penny did her best to avoid staring at the home in front of Luca's parked vehicle because the weight of her actions had finally settled on her shoulders. The man in the driver's seat said nothing as she fidgeted with the gold chain that hung from the rearview mirror. Luca didn't even hint that it was time for her to get out of the car and head inside to see Naz and Roz.

No, he just waited her out.

"I probably made a bigger problem with the caseworker today," Penny muttered. "And the school, right?"

Luca tilted his head her way. "Likely."

Penny rolled her eyes. "Naz and Roz will tell me it's fine. They'll handle it like they always do."

"But that doesn't help, does it?"

Her gaze snapped to his.

He only clarified with, "The guilt, Penny. It doesn't help with the guilt."

Air slipped past her lips in a harsh woosh when she admitted, "No, it doesn't help."

"That should tell you something."

Should it?

"What, then?"

Luca smiled. "That you know they love you … and you love them."

Penny released the chain hanging from the mirror and rested back in the seat. "It's more than just Naz and Roz. You, too. You care about me, too."

"Of course, I do. You have my number, you know how to use it, and you're more than welcome to do so, Penny."

*Right.*

He cared.

Platonically.

As he should.

Penny wished she could say the same but instead when her stare met his again, the truth slipped out before she could stop herself. "I'm not sure I should, actually."

"What, call me? You did today. It didn't end so bad."

Except …

"What happens when I keep calling and you keep showing up?" Penny asked, shrugging and putting her attention on *anything* but the handsome man in the seat next to hers. "I'm already confused about … you. The more you're around, the worse it's gonna get. And it's not your fault, you don't even act like you notice me or how I am when you're around. I've just never—"

"Liked someone before," he murmured.

*God.*

Was it that obvious?

Even he knew?

Penny sighed, saying nothing more except, "I don't know how to deal with any of it, I guess."

"Penny."

She didn't answer.

Didn't even look at him.

Wasn't it bad enough that she went as far as admitting her crush when he hadn't even given her the *suggestion* he felt the same way? She thought so.

"*Penny.* Hey, look at me for a second."

She did.

It was *hard.*

Luca grinned when her stare finally met his, like he was fucking *proud* of her or something. "There you are, huh? Don't be scared to show people who you are, Penny."

"Easier said than done."

"I know. *And* … as for the rest, just know I'm safe. For you, I'm a safe place. Sounds kind of stupid, I know, but it's true. Have a crush on me. *Like me.* Even if it's silly. It's still safe, Penny, because you should also know I'm never going to cross a line."

She nodded.

He was the *good guy.* Every chick flick had one although those men *rarely* looked like Luca. The girl's best friend who was always waiting in the wings to save the day. The unintentional hero who rarely got the girl but didn't seem to need to, either.

Good guys weren't real, though.

Except, she had one.

*Right?*

Luca winked, adding, "Ever, okay?"

"Okay."

Everyone lied.

Or that's what life taught her.

But right then, she believed Luca.

"It's not that I don't trust you," she admitted, grabbing her book bag from the floor of the car. "It's that sometimes I think about what would happen if you did cross a line. I think about it more than I should."

Luca glanced her way, the hard lines of his face softening as his mouth opened to respond. Before he could say anything, Penny leaned over the seat and pressed a quick kiss to his cheek, saying, "Thank you for helping me today."

And then she was gone.

She didn't look back, either.

It was just easier.

# *11.*

*Luca*

LUCA didn't have time to pull out of the driveway before a familiar figure stepped out of the front door. He could still feel Penny's kiss on his cheek. Her words continued banging around in his mind long after she disappeared inside the house. He had no business obsessing over what she did or told him in the first place, but he still did.

Even as Naz approached. He couldn't get it off his goddamn mind while Naz came to stand beside the car, and he rolled the window down to talk.

What was *wrong* with him?

"You okay?" Naz asked.

Luca passed his friend a look from the side, but shrugged it off. "Yeah, man. I'm always good."

Naz nodded, but his attention returned to the front steps leading up to the house. "Any news for me?"

That earned his friend a laugh.

"Depends," he returned.

"On what?"

"What, specifically, you want to know?"

Naz grinned, and shoved his hands into the pockets of his black slacks. "That good of a day, huh?"

"That's one way to put it."

The day had certainly started in a different way than it ended. None of it had been what Luca expected after he got that message from Penny and decided to go pick her up. Then again, when was life ever what he thought it would be?

"Start with whatever, then," Naz said. "We'll work from there."

*Right.*

"Might as well since I'm already here," Luca replied, sighing.

Luca massaged at the tension starting to form between his eyes while his mind went back to the original duty he had that day. Chasing down information on the caseworker that might possibly cause issues for Naz and Roz's guardianship over Penny. He figured that was as good of a place to start as any, surely.

"Your caseworker thing," he muttered.

"What about it?"

That was probably the easiest of all the issues he had to deal with over the day. Finding information on the woman wasn't exactly hard when he only needed to find certain people, ask a few questions, and shove a couple of hundred dollars into the right hands to get the right answers.

*Simple.*

And the information was good, too.

"The woman is in a lot of debt," Luca said. "Surprise, like most Americans. Hers started with student loans and just grew from there. A bad divorce three years ago added another hundred grand on top of what she already owes. Interest isn't *terrible*, but it still isn't great. So, she's pulling more hours than she should on top of an already massive workload. Something to consider as a reason why she might not be seeing Penny's living situation clearly."

"Hmm," Naz hummed under his breath. "Anything else?"

Wasn't there always?

Luca just hadn't gotten there yet.

"The good thing is she doesn't have any kids," Luca said. "The bad thing is she has even more debt from the death of her father two years back … and her mother is currently sick. Cancer, I guess."

Out of the corner of his eye, Luca saw the way Naz flinched at that news. It was subtle, sure, but it still happened. Despite what a lot of people might assume about them—or men like them, for that matter—they did actually have morals. Nobody wanted to kick someone else when they were already down. That shit just wasn't fair.

Some things also couldn't be helped.

Was this one of those?

Luca didn't know. He just did what Naz wanted him to do. He found the information he needed on his problem, and the rest was for his friend to handle the way he wanted. Unless, of course, he asked Luca to deal with that side of things as well.

He would.

Didn't mean he would like it.

"So, I'll fill in the rest of the details," Luca murmured, tipping his head Naz's way to meet his friend's stare. "Her debt just continues growing because she's picking up responsibility left and right. She's overworked, likely underpaid, and it doesn't end when she goes home because guess who just moved in? Right, her mother … currently undergoing treatments for cancer. Shitty thing is, she's *not* wrong about looking into us. You're not the right kind of home for a girl like Penny by all standards."

"Luca—"

"I'm not finished. She's not being abused, though. Everywhere else she's lived after leaving her parents, she actively planned to run away or made suicide attempts. She *has* made progress here. And other than overlooking everything you do business-wise, this home is just fine for Penny. She—and you guys—have done everything asked from school to therapy. The caseworker just sees what's on the surface, the obvious, and she's trying to run with it, so she doesn't miss anything. Crossing t*s* and dotting any i*s*, you know?"

"And probably missing the not-so-obvious from another case that needs actual help," Naz said under his breath. "Wasting my fucking time along with it."

Fair enough.

Luca figured … what could he do now? He did what he needed. Naz had to make the hard choices beyond this point.

"Anyway," Naz said, removing his hands from his pockets to rub his palms together, "it's good to know I've got something to work with there—the debt thing, I mean. Better for me to go a *helpful* route rather than a hurtful one, as my father would say."

"Bribery and blackmail." Luca grinned, the action being returned easily by his best friend. "The very foundations upon which Cosa Nostra was built."

"Oh yeah, this thing of ours … it always comes full circle."

Their jokes eased the tension if anything. Both men laughed, and Luca was grateful for the reprieve from it all. Even if it didn't last long.

It never did.

Naz went right back to business, reminding Luca that the days of their easy banter, before the family business had come along to give the men other things to deal with constantly, were long gone. They fit in what they could, now. Sometimes, that wasn't very damn much.

"As for today," Naz said, turning back to Luca in the car.

"Yeah, *that.*"

"You know the school called."

"Penny will be happy that she doesn't have to fill you in on all the details, then," Luca muttered.

Naz chuckled. "Oh, I'm still gonna get her to talk. It's the only way she does, really."

"Well—"

"What did she tell you?"

"Probably not what the school told you," Luca replied.

Naz arched a brow at that. "What makes you think that?"

"The chances of the little puke she punched telling the truth about *why* she did it? Slim to fuck all, Naz."

"Fair because they didn't even mention something was said when they called. Just that a situation had happened, one they were dealing with, and Penny left the property. I was told they would call back with more information and any consequences to note for Penny's side of things. What was said?"

Yeah …

That was the shitty part.

Luca let out a hard breath, saying, "A guy said something about her father, and *her* … it wasn't really great. She didn't give exact words, and she didn't need to. I assume you can figure it out on your own, too."

Because honestly, not that he would tell Naz, but Luca didn't feel comfortable talking about Penny's business—or the shit that happened to her because of her father—without her presence. Too many people made it their first priority to talk about the girl with little to no consideration for *her* feelings in the matter. He didn't want to be another name on that list.

Not that he thought Naz was the same. His friend was the teenager's guardian. He had every right to discuss his ward and her needs—just like Roz, too. Luca wasn't quite the same, and he was fine with that.

Naz was silent for a long moment.

Eventually, he murmured, "Yeah, probably. *Fuck*."

"Let her be quiet," Luca said, "if that's what she wants. Don't push, man."

"Yeah, you're probably right."

This thing with Penny … it was tricky sometimes. Anything but easy or simple. There was no clear, *right* way to deal with stuff that came up. Luca figured a phone call from the girl once in a while wasn't so bad or hard to handle in the grand scheme. It was Naz and Roz doing the hard work behind the scenes.

Without thanks, too.

Which only made him think of Penny …

It was impossible for him not to think about her if he were being an honest man. She was the catalyst to everything, after all. The very reason both he and Naz were there having a discussion in the first place. If only that was the singular reason for his thoughts drifting back to her, but they weren't.

He worried about her.

All the time.

He hoped she had better days.

And now, with her feelings for him more obvious than before, he found himself considering that, too. Not that he should or planned on acting on the things she told him. It just … *was*. It existed, he knew about, and so he thought about it, too.

Wasn't that human?

Luca didn't know.

Didn't have the first fucking clue.

"She's got a lot of demons," he said more to himself than his friend. "Monsters that chase her all the damn time. How do you help somebody like that?"

"I'm working on that—the monster thing. One at a time, right?"

Luca made a noncommittal noise, but he knew what his friend meant. Hell, more than any of them, Naz made the greatest effort to do something about the people that hurt Penny. He created an entire program to crawl the dark web and hunt the predators down.

The only problem?

"You can't get them all, man," Luca told Naz. "You can't kill every monster out there and certainly not hers. Not the ones in her *mind*, you know what I mean? She's going to have to learn how to slay those on her own. Someday."

Naz nodded. "Maybe, but that day doesn't have to be today."

"Fair enough."

What else needed to be said?

Nothing, he thought.

"Well," Naz said, running a hand through his dark, slicked-back hair as he turned back toward the house, "anything else you want to tell me?"

Luca considered that question.

Was there?

*Yes.*

He knew, without a doubt, that he should tell Naz about Penny's feelings for him. Even if it was nothing more than a silly crush that she wasn't acting on in any real way. Even if she had admitted herself that she didn't know why it existed in the first place or what she planned to do about it. He *should* tell his friend.

Or … the kiss to his cheek.

Any of it.

If anything, so then Naz and Roz could maybe talk to Penny about that sort of thing. Guys. Men. *Him.* Did she even have someone who could help her interpret those feelings? Or the better question, did she *want* to?

That's what kept him quiet.

Penny's wants.

Even if he didn't know what they were, it didn't matter to him. If anything was clear to Luca, it was the fact that so little about Penny's life and mind was private. She had guardians making sure she did everything she needed to do. Teachers and counselors sticking their nose where it didn't belong. A therapist shrinking her head three days a week. Even a fucking caseworker stirring the pot.

Nothing was really … *hers.*

Not without someone else's influence.

Except him.

And her crush.

He also felt like it might be something private for her. She did say she was dealing with it even if she didn't know *how*. That was something, right?

And he was *safe.*

For her.

For this.

He drew a line in the sand, and Luca wouldn't cross it. He wouldn't do shit that proved otherwise, either.

So, did he have anything else to tell Naz?

Luca glanced his friend's way, saying, "Nope. That's about it."

Naz ticked two fingers back, replying, "Good—head out. See you later."

As he backed out of the driveway, Luca was still trying to figure out whether or not he made the right choice.

Nothing was ever simple.

# 12.

*Penny*

THE baby boutique Roz seemed to favor to buy *all the things* for her unborn son was so boujee that the place didn't even have a sign over the door with a name. Instead, they entered the business through a red front door with baskets of roses hanging on either side. The small gold plaque beside a doorbell—in case someone called ahead of time to ask that the store be closed to the general public while they shopped, Roz explained when Penny asked—spelled out the boutique's name in a scripted font.

*The Bebe Palace.*

Cute.

Or something like that.

Penny wasn't one who could spend hours upon hours shopping at any place—never mind one that was so fancy the women waiting inside already had two cups of caffeine-free tea ready in-hand for their newest patrons. Like they had seen them talking just outside the doors and rushed to have everything ready.

She sipped on the fruity flavored hot tea while the women—both in black dresses and matching heels—greeted Roz and fawned over her baby bump. The same thing everyone did whenever Roz was in their presence. It seemed like people couldn't help but be excited over the very idea of a baby.

Maybe … Penny understood that.

She wasn't any better. At least, when it came to Roz's baby. She didn't know anyone else that was pregnant, and she really didn't care to. But there was definitely *something* about Roz's pregnancy that excited her, especially now that they were reaching the end.

Because soon, *he* would be here.

Baby Cross, that was.

Penny couldn't wait to meet the little guy she had watched grow through sonogram pictures and doctor updates. And as Roz broke away from the smiling women in the entrance of the boutique to head for a nearby rack of baby clothes, she knew exactly why that was, too.

For once, she felt … *involved.* Welcomed, even. A part of something that was bigger than her, if that made any sense at all. It wasn't like she asked for a family—of sorts—when Naz and Roz took her in after everything that happened, but they did and they gave her a home in the process.

Maybe without meaning to.

What did it matter?

*It happened.*

Penny was terrified someone might try to take it away from her, too. These people … she loved them, and she didn't want to be forced to leave them, either.

"Look at *this*," Roz squealed, snatching the item off the rack that must have caught her attention enough to pull her in that direction. She spun around, holding the black leather jacket—sized appropriately for a small infant—high for everyone to see. And despite the women who preened over the item, telling Roz it was one of the cutest they had in the shop, she only looked to Penny for a reply. "What do you think?"

She knew what *Roz* thought about it, and she wasn't wrong. "It's perfect. Looks just like the one Naz walks around wearing most of the time."

And it did.

Right down to the silver buttons and hardware. She was sure the unborn baby's father would be over the moon when he saw it. Other than tiny Doc Marten boots, Naz hadn't brought home very much for the baby saying, *They're all gonna buy too much like they always do.*

He wasn't wrong. The baby shower was weeks away, and people were already sending gifts in lieu of their ability to attend the party. Which meant the entry to the house was full of boxes and gift bags constantly. They changed every day, too.

Penny had finally decided on her gift for Roz, but it was more like a gift for both. She still needed to get something specific to finish the gift, so now it was one less thing for Penny to obsess over, anyway. She wasn't going to be able to find the thing she needed here, though.

Roz nodded, peering down at the item while she still held it out in front of her. "Right? I'm getting it for sure."

That was all the women needed to hear. One stepped forward to take the jacket from Roz with a promise of having it ready at the front when she was ready to leave. The other woman slinked off when Roz said they were fine to shop alone. And that was how Penny and Roz found themselves wandering through the baby boutique.

Rack after rack of expensive baby clothes—and other items—stared back at Penny. It was kind of overwhelming, if only because she couldn't figure out how people justified paying a hundred dollars for nothing more than swaddling wrap when the baby was only going to grow out of it within a couple of months.

That seemed like … a waste.

But hey, it wasn't her money.

And she wasn't a *baby* person.

Except for Roz's baby.

That was different.

"You're still good with the baby shower, right?" Roz asked from the other side of a rack filled with expensive baby jeans featuring tags with names she recognized. Since when did Gucci make baby clothes? "I mean, it's going to be *a lot* of people, Penny, and I don't want you to be uncomfortable. So just let us know if you need—"

"It'll be fine."

*Lies.*

The idea of being in a house with at least a hundred or more people—a lot of which she wouldn't know from a hole in the ground—terrified her to no end. But she was also trying this new thing where, at least when it came to people she gave a shit about, she actually *tried* to think of someone other than herself.

Roz's shower was about *Roz.*

Not Penny.

Or her dislike of people.

"Even so," Roz said, giving her a pointed look, "if you do need five minutes to breathe at the baby shower, just take it. No one is going to be offended."

Penny smiled. "Yeah, okay."

Roz prattled on about the shower while they continued flipping through the rack. Not about anything too serious—certainly not what happened just a couple of days before at the school. In fact, her guardians barely said anything about the fight.

She wondered why.

Eventually, Penny just blurted out, "Are we not going to talk about what happened at school, or …?"

Roz didn't look away from a pair of toddler-sized jeans as she asked, "Do we need to?"

"Shouldn't we?"

"Well, we're handling it. The meeting with the school *and* caseworker—because apparently they decided to include her this time around—has been set. There's not much else we can do until that happens."

Penny didn't even try to hide her scowl when she said, "That bitch just wants to move me in with someone else."

Did she sound whiny? Petty? Like every other teenage girl in the world that was selfish and self-absorbed?

*Yep.*

She also didn't care. Nothing she said was untrue.

Roz gave her a smile from across the rack, making Penny say, "Well, I'm right. And I'm seventeen, eighteen in a few months, so why can't I just pick where I want to live?"

"If it came down to that," Roz replied, "the judge would consider your input."

A *judge.*

Christ.

Penny didn't want to deal with the law any more than she had to. Once—for her father's charges and a trial that didn't happen—was enough. She still felt like the system hadn't done very much for her at the end of the day. She wasn't about to jump at the chance to trust it to do the right thing a second time around.

"And," Roz added, hooking the hanger attached to the jeans back on the rack, "other than getting through the meeting, I don't think we're going to have too many more problems from the school or the caseworker. They emailed a list of requirements for you leading up to it—like attending your therapy—but you do all of that, anyway. Don't worry. We'll deal with it."

Yeah, they always did.

Penny might like to start doing things for them, too.

But how?

• • •

Penny was all too aware that the last therapy session before she returned to school for the meeting with the caseworker and principal was important. No doubt, a determining factor to a lot of things that still felt like they were just hanging up in the air. So, she was on her best behavior despite still not wanting to be there in the first place.

Her therapist asked questions—she answered them. The doctor wanted to talk, like she always did, so Penny made every effort to try.

It was the least she could do.

*Right?*

Anything to make this better.

"And things are going well at home?" Dr. Tangler asked. "Roz must be quite far along in her pregnancy. How's that changing things?"

"Everyone's excited," Penny replied.

The woman stared at her over the rim of her glasses. "Even you?"

"Especially me."

"Really."

It wasn't even a question.

That made Penny's brow dip when she asked, "Why wouldn't I be excited about the baby? Never even held a baby before, but I don't know … I just want to meet him. We all talk about him like he's already here, anyway. Be nice to actually have him here, you know?"

Dr. Tangler smiled. "I do know, yes."

"Do you have kids?"

"Two. Both teenagers so they're … not quite babies."

"Oh."

"You know, that's the first time you've asked about me in all of our sessions together," the therapist said, shrugging. "Why?"

Penny didn't really have to think about it. "I was curious."

"About someone else."

"Why not?"

"It's not a bad thing. It's … a good indicator that things are changing around you. Maybe *inside* you, too. You're starting to see a bigger picture and not your immediate circumstance. You're looking toward things that are coming in the *future*. Instead of just trying to deal with what's happening right now. And I'm sure," the woman added before Penny could open her mouth and contradict what she said, "that you still have moments where it's one day at a time—or one breath at a time, even—but it's not *all the time*. Do you realize how big that is?"

She hadn't.

Not until the doctor pointed it out.

"They've made a place for me," Penny replied, "that lets me do … *that*. I guess. Naz and Roz, I mean. They don't ask for much except for me to try. And so I do. Not that I wanted to at first, but then I did. For them, mostly."

"And now?"

"More for me."

The therapist nodded. "A safe place. They're your safe place. It's normal, Penny. You went from living in a very unstable, unhealthy situation with people who only caused you pain to the complete opposite. Isn't it time to leave what used to be where it is—in the past? Aren't you ready to leave that place now?"

Was she?

"I just … want to be here," Penny murmured.

"Here as in alive or with them?"

"With them."

Naz.

And Roz.

Their soon-to-be born baby boy. The family that welcomed her. *All of them.*

Luca, too. Even if the strange connection she felt to him was just something she had made up in her own mind.

"And alive," Penny added quieter.

Tangler smiled again. "Each person in your life—at the moment—has given you a reason to want to be here. Eventually, that teaches you to find reasons why *you* want to be here as well. Beyond them—it's about you and your needs."

"That's scary, actually."

"Why because you need someone else?"

"Maybe."

But also, because she couldn't remember a time when she hadn't been suicidal; or when those dark thoughts chased her day and night. She hadn't cut in months. She hadn't had an active suicide plan since her last attempt in Europe. Were things perfect? No, but … Penny had come to learn life wasn't about creating perfection. It was about finding the perfect moments amongst everything else.

"Are you happy?" her therapist asked. "Is that what you're trying to figure out?"

Was she?

Penny blinked, replying, "I'm not … depressed. I don't want to die."

"But are you *happy*?"

"I'm not sure I know what being happy looks like."

Honesty was the best policy, right?

"Despite how it might look from your perspective like it's something you can't obtain," her therapist said, "happiness is something most people fall into naturally. In your case, it's yet another thing for you to learn, Penny. As long as you're willing to keep trying—and clearly you are—then it'll all fall into place. You simply have to give it time to do so."

Well …

She would certainly keep it in mind.

At this point, what did she have to lose?

Another thought smacked Penny like a slap to the face. *A lot, actually.*

Now more than ever, Penny had a lot to lose. Maybe that's what scared her more than anything else ever had.

As the second hand ticked down the final minute of their session, Penny stood from the chair she always used while she was there, ready to leave. Dr. Tangler offered her another smile, but this one felt … different.

"And for the record," the therapist told her as she shrugged on her coat, "despite the impression you might have left here with after our last discussion, I am going to recommend that you stay in the care of your current guardians. It's where you have been—and will do—your best. Anyone who can't see as much is a fool and isn't looking hard enough."

*Good.*

One more thing to get through, then.

That's all that mattered to Penny.

# *13.*

## *Penny*

LEADING up to the meeting at the school with the principal and Penny's caseworker—who decided when they walked into the office that everyone should call her Amanda—Roz continued to tell her not to worry about anything. Naz wasn't any different. Despite how they tried to calm her fears, she still headed into that meeting feeling like the whole world was about to crash down around her.

She sat between Naz and Roz on a chair that didn't look—or feel—nearly as comfortable as the ones provided to her guardians for the meeting. The principal observed them from her seat behind the desk. All the while, the caseworker flipped through her file, seemingly fine with being silent while the principal laid out every single issue that had been noted about Penny since the last time she was there.

Yeah, it was still a whole list.

Penny could apologize …

It was probably the right time.

But she didn't.

"However," the principal said, making Penny look up from her hands to meet the woman's gaze from across the desk, "we're also aware that this latest problem was not entirely … Penny's fault."

"She shouldn't have hit him, though," Roz said to her left. "Right, Penny?"

"Well—"

"*Penny*," Naz murmured.

"I could have handled it better," she settled on saying.

*After* she hit him.

He did deserve that.

"And I apologize for Caleb's insensitive words that I'm sure hurt and did nothing to help you with moving beyond the things you're currently dealing with, Penny," Mrs. Tippens added. "Taking all of that into account, and everything else, we've decided that a two-week suspension is most appropriate—"

"Two weeks—"

"*And*," the principal said, arching a brow to silence Roz, "while it's what we would do to any student for the same behavior Penny has shown, this is also to her benefit. It will give her more time at home with people who clearly care about her and have been making progress with her where it *counts*. I do notice those things despite what you two might think. During her two-week suspension, she is expected to do daily online classes. It'll allow her to still graduate on time. When the suspension is up, she can continue classes online and report to the school twice a week for two hours of in-class work."

*Hey.*

Penny didn't mind that at all. She would have done that from the beginning had someone given her the option. For the most part, they kept pushing her to be *at* school more than outside of it. Like being around people and other students her age would … help.

It hadn't.

"As long as she passes her classes and finals," the principal continued, "then she will be allowed to walk in the graduation ceremony with her class. Or we can mail her diploma, but I will leave that decision up to her, and *you*. That's all I have to say except, Penny …"

"Yeah?"

Mrs. Tippens smiled softly. "I *am* trying to give you the legroom you need to move and make this work. *Please*, make it work."

Fair enough.

"I will."

"Good. I'll allow you four to finish this meeting without me as I have other things to attend. Miss Carine, you can take my seat if you would like, or stand. That's up to you."

The principal gathered the items she wanted from her desk, and then left the room without a glance over her shoulder at the people she left behind. The caseworker, Amanda Carine, didn't take the seat behind the desk that had been offered to her. Instead, she rounded the front of the desk and leaned her backside against the edge as she opened a folder and pretended like she was actually reading the contents inside.

Penny knew it was for show. Especially when the woman started listing things without even looking down at the papers inside the folder.

"Lack of willingness to participate in school, *or* therapy, even if she does regularly attend both. Fights at school. Issues with teachers, students, and anyone within breathing distance. Now, a suspension can be added to the list of issues that have cropped up since Penny moved into your home as well, Mr. Donati and Miss Puzza. Also." The caseworker glanced Roz's way specifically, her gaze narrowing when she said, "I see the two of you still aren't married. I thought that was happening sooner rather than lat—"

"We're not here to discuss our marriage plans," Naz spoke up. "But by all means, continue with the other bullshit. We will listen to that at least."

"Excuse me?"

Roz sighed, looking like she was over the entire day. Being heavily pregnant, anybody could understand why. "Penny has also managed to maintain a decent grade average despite the trouble she's found at school—and not all of that trouble was her own fault, either. She *does* attend therapy, and even her therapist says she's made progress during sessions as far as opening up is concerned. We've not had a *single* incident at our home that needed attention. No violence, no self-harm … nothing. She even plays the piano again, of course, when she wants to. But I think it's important to note that Penny hadn't even touched piano keys for almost two years before she came into our care. Not without being *forced* to, anyway."

"And what does any of that have to do with *this*?" the caseworker asked, tipping the file in their direction like the lists she had inside of there should mean shit.

"Well," Roz replied, "I think it's only fair that if you're going to name every bad thing that's happened, it's equally important for you to list the positive, too. Weigh the good against the bad, so to speak. Because really, the only issue that's caused us *real* problems with Penny since she's come into our care is you."

"What—"

"You," Naz repeated for Roz, although stronger that time. "Penny has no issue with causing a scene when she's unhappy in a situation. As your file probably shows. And the only thing that's truly upset her progress with us in these past couple of months is your incessant need to step in and suggest we weren't capable of taking care of her. *That* upset her, in turn, causing us problems that we had to fix."

"You have to understand," the caseworker tried to say, "that I only see what is shown to me. I'm also looking out for the best interests of the two of you as well. You're both young, you have a baby on the way, and Penny is …"

The woman glanced her way. She *did* smile, but it didn't feel entirely true. Like most people, this woman looked at her and saw a mountain of problems that she didn't know how to begin fixing let alone *help*. Naz and Roz weren't the same. They didn't try to fix shit for Penny. They let her do it on her own and when she needed them, they were there.

*That's* why she wanted them.

And to stay with them.

"Is *she* appropriate for your current circumstances—that's all I want you two to consider at this time," Amanda said, closing the folder.

"Do we ignore that literally everyone except you has said she's better with us than without?" Naz asked. "Her therapist. The school. Even her physician that has only seen her three times, and one of those were for a check-up. We just, what, pretend like their recommendations don't exist?"

The caseworker exhaled heavily. "Yes, everything seems to fall right into place for any Donati in this city, doesn't it?"

For the first time during the entire meeting—because Penny promised Naz and Roz she would stay quiet and let them handle this entire thing—she spoke out of turn, but only to tell the caseworker, "I want to stay where I am. I want to stay with Naz and Roz."

"Considering the circumstances, I don't think they're the right place for you to be, Penny."

And?

"Well, I do," Penny replied sharper than she intended.

"*I* believe you would be better placed where you could receive more specialized care," Amanda said, shrugging like she didn't care to hear a thing Penny had to say about it. "And that's really what it boils down to."

Oh, really?

Penny had tried hard since coming to live with Naz and Roz to keep her more spiteful and cruel tendencies under control. But before them, her mean streak had been infamous with anyone who knew her well enough to stay far the fuck away. Did she get stuck with a roommate she didn't want at one of her private schools? Fine—she made it impossible for the girl to even breathe the same air. A boy spreading rumors or making jokes with his dumbass friends? All right—let the games begin.

She could ruin a life.

She *had.*

Penny was also just mean when she wanted to be—for no other reason than she could be. People made it too easy and when she didn't like them to begin with, she felt little to no guilt about doing what she had to do.

Except she tried with Naz and Roz. *Hard.* After all, they only wanted to help her and so, she really couldn't justify being more trouble in their life than she already was. Yet, for the first time in more months than she cared to count, Penny felt that all too familiar pull of her vindictive side coming out to play as she stood from the chair. Every gaze in the room turned on her, including her guardians, but she only stared at the caseworker standing in front of the principal's desk.

"Do you know what used to happen when someone tried to put me in places with more *specialized care?*" Penny asked, twisting the words with enough venom that she hoped the woman knew she wasn't fucking around. "First it was my parents—they tossed me into whatever private school they could just to hide me away. But no worries, I always made my way back one way or another. One problem at a time. But then it was the schools … I needed more structure, they said. I needed a stricter environment. Whatever. I started cutting deeper until I was doing real damage, and they didn't have a choice but to move me again."

Penny laughed, the sound tired to even her own ears. "See, then they all just gave up. Institutions and mental health wards were the only things left, and even that shit didn't take. So, let's make sure we all understand where each of us stands here, Miss Carine—or do you want me to call you Amanda? Never mind, don't answer. I honestly don't give a fuck. I like where I am. I don't cut, I'm finally *safe*, and for once, I'm happy. As long as you understand that if you remove me from Naz and Roz's home things are going to get a lot harder for you where I'm concerned, that's all that really matters."

The caseworker's jaw dropped.

Penny smiled back. "Everything clear?"

She didn't actually wait for a response.

"Great," Penny said, snatching her coat from the back of the chair. "I'll be waiting outside."

She turned to slide between the chairs and head out of the office.

"Penny," Roz started to say.

On the other side, where Naz had been seated, he quietly said, "Just let her go, babe."

Penny didn't stop long enough to say thanks. She didn't want to leave just because she showed her mean streak. No, she simply wanted distance between herself and the caseworker because she truly couldn't stand the sight of the woman at the moment. It had been a long couple of months since Amanda started suggesting Penny be removed from the home, and she finally hit her limit.

At least she knew it.

Wasn't removing herself from the equation—even if she *did* throw a tiny fit first—some growth? Penny thought so. But who knew?

She didn't bother to stop and talk to the principal waiting outside the office with her assistant, instead opting to slip past the women and leave the outer section of the reception as well. In the hallway, empty of students as classes were in, she found a bench and sat. Pulling the phone from her bag, she stuck EarPods into her ears and within seconds, music filtered through the small speakers straight to her brain.

Everything disappeared, then.

It was just Penny, and the piano.

She still didn't play as much as she used to—or as much as she should, according to Roz. And when she did sit down to play, it was only because she wanted to now. The piano wouldn't be a source of pain for her … not if she had anything to say about it.

It was a few minutes later when a familiar presence joined her on the bench. She didn't even need to glance up from her lap to know it was Naz just by the scent of his cologne. Out of the corner of her eye, she watched him fold his hands in his lap and lean forward a bit. At first, he said nothing, seemingly content to sit in silence beside Penny until Roz joined them.

Where was Roz, anyway?

Despite the music filtering through the ear pods, she still heard Naz clearly when he did finally speak. Only to say to her, "You know throwing threats doesn't actually help us here. You don't need me to tell you that, Penny."

She shrugged.

What did he want her to say?

"Even if it is only you trying to get your way," he added, chuckling like he found the whole thing amusing.

She dared to glance his way.

Naz grinned. "You don't need to attempt to blackmail the caseworker—emotional blackmail never works very well, anyway, unless it's someone that really gives a fuck about you. It wasn't needed. The blackmail, I mean. I already had that side of things handled. I went the bribery route, of course."

Penny opened her mouth to respond. He arched a brow to keep her questions silent.

"She put on a good show, though, didn't she?" he asked.

"I hate her."

"Yeah, us too." Then, Naz stood from the bench, adding, "You're not going anywhere. I promised, remember?"

"I remember."

"Good. I always keep those."

Penny still wondered … "Does this mean everything goes back to normal now? Is this over?"

Naz smirked, saying, "Well, normal for us, anyway."

Yeah, but she liked their normal.

Didn't that count for something?

# *INTERLUDE: 2.*

*Present Day …*

"THEN why did you leave?" Cross tipped his chin higher, that sharp gaze of his looking Penny up and down without pause. *Considering*, she knew. Considering her. Waiting to find her lie. Like maybe he could sense it before it even passed her lips. *Could he?* "I'm little, even though I don't like it, but they know I'm not little, too, in some ways. So they're careful when they talk. But they still do or I still hear it. You were with my parents for more than a year. You said you loved me—they loved *you*, I know. And then you left. *Why?*"

If only Penny dared to close her eyes, she imagined that she could pretend this was a conversation between two adults. Certainly not one between a grown woman and a five-year-old boy. It was a strange thing to hear wisdom in the voice of a child. She had to wonder if that was how people felt talking to her as a child that had seen and knew things that were far beyond her comprehension.

"That's not an easy answer," Penny replied in a whisper.

"The truth is always easy," Cross replied, folding his leather-clad arms over his small chest. There was something to be said about being stared down by a child. Especially when it felt like that child was also judging you. "Because people lie—*all the time*. Everyone does it. But they always have to think about it, make sure it *sounds* right … it's a choice to lie. Like Uncle Luca says, shit's a process."

Penny coughed out a laugh alongside muttering, "He says *what?*"

Cross rolled his eyes. "He says a lot of stuff. That one is right, though. The truth just *is*. Telling it sometimes hurts, or changes things, but it is still the truth. Right?"

"You see things in a very black and white way, don't you?"

"Kind of."

"Is it easier that way?" she asked. "Easier to understand why you get to be this way … and everyone else is the way they are, too?"

Honestly curious, she waited for his reply.

The little boy blinked, surprise darting over his young face for a split second. "No one's ever asked me that before."

"No?"

"No."

Penny shoved her hands into the pocket of her black windbreaker, telling him, "Maybe because they don't know how—they can't understand anyway."

"Maybe. And it's not easy. It just is."

Penny didn't point out how he said the same thing about the truth. Whether he knew it or not, yes, he did deal with his strange uniqueness in a yes or no, black or white manner because it was easier for him than delving deeper.

It showed his youth. Possibly one of the few things that did. What he lacked in actual age and experience, he simplified things down to just *being*.

Cross lifted his brow and smiled, a flash of arrogance showing in the action that almost had her laughing when he added, "But you still didn't tell me why, and I didn't forget."

*Smart kid.*

In a lot of damn ways.

"Because I had to," she said, knowing all too well it wouldn't satisfy him, but it also wasn't a lie. "I left because I had to."

"That's …" Cross's brow furrowed. "Well, *why*?"

"Because it was the right thing to do. The only thing I could do."

"Do *what*, though?"

"Leave," she replied.

Cross let out a huff, gaze narrowing in on her again with a new gleam. "I know what you're doing."

Penny grinned. "Yeah?"

"Saying the truth."

"But?"

"Without details," he said, defeated.

She only shrugged.

*Fair was fair.*

Her godson might have card tricks of his own—although being able to read people at his age was way more amazing than just a *card trick*—but she had a few, too.

Cross shook his head. "Uncle Luca told them you were different."

That made her pause.

All over.

Penny turned to stone at just the mere mention of Luca. She had been content to come back to this place, say goodbye and *hope*, and then leave it all behind if that's what came of her choices. She'd forced herself to stop thinking about the people she kept leaving behind, too. Sacrifices had to be made, after all.

That didn't stop it from hurting.

Cross observed her in silent stillness, waiting for a reply from her that wouldn't come. It couldn't. "He likes you a lot, too."

Penny's throat flexed when she managed to ask, "What?"

"Uncle Luca. When people miss things—things that mean *something*—their eyes change. More distant. Like they're looking at something far away. Something I can't see. You did what he did when he told them he found you. But you did it now because I talked about him. See, same thing."

This kid was … something else.

She also couldn't afford to stand there and keep talking to him even though every single molecule in her being wanted to do exactly that. He was amazing. It took a single conversation with the kid to realize just how much she had missed out on where he was concerned.

"I really should go," Penny said, moving a step deeper into the forest. The same way she had come.

The shout from behind her made her next step hesitate.

"*Cross*! Get back to the house, son! Time to eat!"

# 14.

*Luca*

BEING ten minutes late wasn't anything unusual for Luca, but tonight wasn't the night for his tardiness, and he knew it. It was why he tried his very best to sneak out of the lecture for one of his college classes—he had dropped down to two classes a week that only required him to show up two days a week, the rest could be done online—but that hadn't worked out. Instead, he ended up getting *another* lecture from the professor about the importance of education and wasting the time of others.

Like he needed to be told.

*Again.*

By someone else.

So, all his efforts to arrive early—if not on time—for his best friend and sister's baby shower was for nothing. Because the world seemed to enjoy having a good laugh at Luca's fucking expense. Every step forward he made was greeted with a kick right back in his former place.

*Sort of.*

No one seemed to notice Luca arriving late when he stepped inside the mansion where Roz and Naz's families decided to have the party. He could also tell, just with a quick look at the people milling in the grand entry, that he wasn't *technically* late. The quiet murmurs and the way people turned to stare his way expectantly only to shrug and go back to their conversations said the guests of the hour had yet to arrive.

So, he was on time.

Kind of.

But barely.

He recognized most of the faces—people from the Puzza side, but *a lot* from Naz's family. Waving a hand to say hello to the people who called to him from across the entry, he didn't bother with more. Heading into the coatroom, he shrugged off the tweed coat he'd thrown on over the blazer he managed to keep from getting wrinkled in the back of his car. Alongside the button-down and slacks he tossed in just for good measure.

He knew better than to show up wearing jeans and a hoodie. He didn't go for the whole three-piece look for the baby shower, forgoing a tie and vest just because that shit hadn't been specified. If he could avoid the whole suit and tie get-up, then he would by whatever means necessary.

Despite what men around him seemed to think about proper dress wear for people of their name and status, he just didn't care. Or liked it all that much. Too confining for his tastes, honestly.

By the time Luca stepped out of the coatroom, the entry had cleared of guests. Well, mostly. A few remained but they were halfway in and out, standing on the threshold of the entry to the ballroom where he could already see the pale blue and white decorations hanging down from the high ceilings.

Balloon archways.

Tulle everywhere.

White lights, probably tall centerpieces on every table, and that was only the beginning. No one threw a party quite like their families did. Even Luca knew that—it was something they took pride in never mind the fact that very rarely did they invite event planners to help.

The women liked it, though.

And it always looked great.

Fixing the middle button on his blazer, Luca glanced up at the same time to see a familiar face making her way down one of two curving staircases in the grand entrance. Penny, that was.

In a black dress with long sleeves and a skirt that fell to her knees, the item hugged her form in all the right places. Even *he* noticed, not that he should. In his excuse, it was the first time he saw her in anything other than sweats or jeans, and an oversized hoodie. The dress was *none* of that.

She looked older.

The smile on her face helped, too.

She was *smiling*. Something she rarely did, although he did notice she was doing it more often lately.

Penny found him in the space, her smile stretching wider as she raised her hand to wave. He only nodded back, but it wasn't her fault. The man approaching him from the side grabbed his attention, and it took every ounce of effort for Luca not to frown at the sight of his father.

Because Zeke *was* frowning.

"You're late," his father muttered coming to stand directly in front of Luca. Zeke folded his arms over his chest, the silver of his vest matching the silk pocket square *and* tie. "You know tonight is important, Luca."

"Are the guests of the hour here?" he returned easily.

He wasn't doing this with his father. Not tonight.

Zeke pursed his lips. "No, and that only means you're *lucky*."

Lucky for what?

Avoiding yet *another* lecture?

Luca didn't think so.

"Lecture ran late," he explained. "I'm already behind on enough shit as it is; forgive me for trying to play catch up where I can."

Zeke sighed, and opened his mouth to speak again. Luca knew, before the words even passed his father's lips, what the man planned to say. It was the same shit he always said whenever his son dared to bring up the fact he was *still* trying where the law school thing was concerned.

*A waste of time.*

*Wasting your potential.*

*Family … family … family.*

"Is it time, Luca?" Zeke asked.

Luca's brow dipped. "Time for what?"

"To make a decision. College or the family business?"

Ah, there it was.

"You have to figure out where your priorities are," Zeke added, repeating the same thing with the usual tone-deafness that Luca had come to expect from his father when it came to things that were important to his son. "You're spread thin … it's starting to show in little ways. You have to decide whether you want to be a lawyer or a made man. Hell, your mother and I haven't even seen you in a *month*."

"Why I can't be both?"

Because that was all Luca heard in his father's statements. That there was no option for both in his case. He could only be one or the other. The thing was … he wasn't big on being told no or what he could or couldn't do. It only encouraged him to try harder in that respect.

Or to just do it for the hell of it.

Out of spite, even.

"Do you really think—"

"Has he been handling all of it?" came a new—but familiar—voice.

Luca hadn't even noticed Cross's approach until the man was right there, standing next to Zeke. Except, the boss of the Donati *famiglia* didn't even bother looking his way. Instead, he stared at Luca's father, waiting for the answer to the question he asked.

Zeke's jaw flexed. "Cross—"

"Is he, friend?"

"I'm not sure I would say he's *handling* it all … or not well," Zeke clarified. "He's behind in every aspect."

Ouch.

"Mostly school," Luca admitted when Cross glanced his way. "Work, not so much."

That was a priority. It had to be because people—like Naz—depended on Luca to be where they needed him to be when they wanted him there. He made sure his friend never had to wonder what he was doing. If he said he would do shit, then he was there to do it when he promised he would.

His word was everything.

Sometimes, it felt like it was the only thing he had left.

"So, he's doing what he's supposed to, then," Cross said, shrugging when

Zeke gave the man a look that voiced his displeasure silently. "He *is*, Zeke, by all accounts. As long as others aren't suffering where he isn't right on the ball, then you can't say he's hurting anyone but himself."

"Maybe that is what I'm worried about. Did you consider that before you decided to step in on a private conversation between my son and I?"

Ah, shit.

*Awkward.*

Cross and Zeke stared one another down, years of friendship passing between the two quiet men as they considered each other. Even Luca knew they were having a conversation—one without words—that he wasn't privy to. They had been doing this same thing for years. This wasn't new.

Spinning the black onyx ring on his finger, Cross eventually broke the silence first, murmuring to Zeke, "I understand your frustrations—with me and him—but sometimes I don't think you hear the damage you do with your words. They hear a lot more than they see or speak, Zeke. And if he hasn't actually failed at managing the life he's chosen, then you shouldn't tell him he will before it's even happened. You're manifesting destiny. Let him hear it enough, and he'll do exactly what you say he will."

"Cross—"

"He's not like the rest of them. He's not Rosalynn, or Naz … or me and you. He is *him*. Let him figure out what works for him," Cross said, finally letting go of his ring to open his arms wide. "Even if it's not the path you might have taken in his shoes. The same way we were allowed to do as young men. Fair?"

Zeke sighed, nodding once. "Fair."

Was that … it?

Cross moved to step away, but stopped only long enough to hear Luca say, "Thanks."

Over his shoulder, the man replied, "Don't mention it."

Zeke's gaze came back to Luca but before his father could say anything more, Katya and Catherine—Naz's mother—came rushing into the entry.

"They're coming—they're at the gates!"

The guests of the hour had arrived, it seemed. Any family business could wait.

• • •

"Congrats, Roz," Luca murmured against the top of his little sister's head.

His sister beamed. For him, yeah, but also because the crowd gathered in front of the massive, beautifully decorated backdrop were taking pictures. Of them. The siblings, but also a million other shots, too.

With a variety of interchanging family, with the pregnant lady, or of the expectant father … with his mother, *her* mother, and anyone else that decided to join in. Luca was about done with the pictures because he had done his part already and was told as much by Roz, but he'd do a few more.

For his sister.

Of course.

And hell, if she could stand there basically nine months pregnant for a million pictures, then who cared if his shoes pinched?

Roz swung around to hug Luca's middle with a squeeze for the next picture, and he laughed before kissing her on the top of her head.

Her shampoo was still the same as it had been when they were teenagers. Strawberries and cream. He connected that scent—*anywhere*—to three things: family, love, and his sister. Despite being the older of the two, he could count on one hand the number of times Roz actually let him *feel* like her older brother. Maybe it was that singular year that separated the two, but it really did feel like they grew up together.

Staring down at his sister, Luca let out a slow breath before telling her, "At some point, you shot far ahead of me, huh? Went out and grabbed a career, and then started a whole family while I was … when did I look away, Roz?"

Because shit …

"Remember when we were still kids and when I started getting my own friends, you made me let you hang out with us because, as you said, 'I gave you friends *first*!' Or some shit like that. You weren't wrong, though."

Roz grinned, a line of wetness glistening in her eyes. "Don't make me cry. You will *never* hear the end of it when they have to stop the pictures just to fix my makeup."

"None of you need that shit, anyway."

And it was true.

The men around them?

Loved all their women—unapologetically. A lot of things could be said about a good many of them—they were heroes to some and villains to many more—but no one could say they didn't love their women with everything they had.

Luca had a lot of problems with his own father—or maybe it was just the growing pains of life that he was trying to get through—but he was also grateful for Zeke more than he could explain. The man that drove him crazy with expectations was also the same man who, without excuse, treated the women in his life with utmost respect and *loyalty*.

The same way he did for Cosa Nostra. Like the women who allowed them to share their lives were worth the same oath that they coveted to only those who could be *made*. The importance of those things wasn't lost on Luca.

"Turn and smile again, guys!" someone shouted from the crowd of semi-pro photogs. Luca smirked as they turned, amused at his own dry humor.

"That's *not* a smile, Luca," he heard his mother call.

*Fuck.*

Luca smiled alongside his sister for another round of shots. That's when Roz decided to tell him, "You and Penny … you'll be good godparents for him. And Luca?"

He turned her way. "Yeah?"

"I didn't shoot ahead of you. Right now, we just want different things. And there's nothing wrong with not being sure what it is you want, either."

Trust his sister to be the one person who saw Luca like cellophane. Completely see-through. She always knew what was in his heart … another by-product of the two of them growing up together as they did.

Almost twins.

But not quite.

Luca didn't get the chance to thank his sister for—once again—being absolutely wonderful. Someone in the crowd of the picture taking guests must have noticed Naz trying to sneak by because in the next thirty seconds … his best friend stood beside him for the next round of pictures.

"This is never going to end," Luca whispered through a smile.

"Why do you think we put this party off as long as we could?" Naz asked back, faking his own grin for the crowd and talking through his teeth. "We used Penny as an excuse, for the last couple of months, because it really *wasn't* an excuse at that point. To be fair."

Luca chuckled. "Nah, I get it."

Someone—one of their mothers, probably—must have noticed the guys were getting a little beyond their *give-a-fuck* line for the picture-taking. "Give them a break, guys! Sweets are coming!"

"Holy … thank *fuck*," Naz muttered, immediately turning around to face the backdrop instead of the guests. There, he could roll his eyes. Luca couldn't help but laugh at the sight. "Sorry—you know we're grateful but *shit* … this is a whole day thing, and we're tired."

"Don't apologize. Remember my graduation?"

Naz nodded, grinning. "But damn, they let us party for *days* after."

Yeah.

They had.

"Evened itself out," Luca agreed.

Naz sighed, turning back around with Luca at his side, so they could observe the guests fawning over silver trays of sweets that had been brought in during their distraction. "You know, I always thought our boys would be like us growing up … together, I mean. Better jump on that, huh?"

Luca sucked in a hiss. "Kids?"

He didn't even hide the way his voice raised at the very idea.

"Not yet," he added.

Naz barked out a laugh, clapping Luca on his back at the same time. "I was kidding—knew that would take a breath out of you."

Luca shook his head. "Fuck you."

"Had to do it."

"On a real level, though?"

Naz glanced his way, asking, "Yeah?"

"I can't fucking wait to meet him."

*His godson.*

Naz's boy.

Fuck, yeah.

Little Cross.

Luca might not be anywhere near ready for kids of his own—maybe he wouldn't ever be; it had never been something he gave much thought—but he couldn't wait to meet his nephew. That kid would want for *nothing*. Not with him around, anyway.

Naz smiled, almost like he knew what Luca was thinking when he replied, "I know."

"Naz, come try this!" Roz called, coming their way with a tart in her hand. "They're the kind you like."

Luca shrugged when he told his friend, "Hey, no hard feelings but I'm gonna sneak out of the way before they get started on the photo thing again, okay?"

"No worries, man."

Naz went for Roz while Luca headed off to the side. It wasn't just the photo thing that made him want to move away from the backdrop set up. He just happened to take note of Penny grabbing a gift box from the massive pile of presents at the other side of the ballroom before she darted out a rear entryway.

He wasn't sure what *that* was about.

But he intended to find out.

• • •

"What are you doing?"

Penny swung around in the hallway, her shitty attempt to hide the gift box at her back doing *nothing* to help her case when she replied, too fast, "Nothing."

"Oh?" Luca pointed at the bit of bow he could still see peeking out from behind her. "Then, what's that right there?"

"Nothing."

"*Penny*."

Despite how mature her dress made her appear, she couldn't hide her age when she rolled her eyes and made a face. "Fine. It's … my gift."

She brought the gift box with the silky looking bow back around to her front for him to see.

"Your gift, or Roz's?"

"*My* gift that I bought for Roz," Penny clarified.

Then, she corrected that again with, "Bought and made, sort of."

"What?"

"What?" she asked back.

Fuck.

Even Luca was confused.

"What are you *doing*?" he decided to ask, figuring going back to the beginning was a good starting point.

What could they lose?

Penny frowned, her grip on the box tightening as she glanced down at it. "Okay, don't judge me but … did you see some of the stuff out there for the *gifts*? A vintage carriage? There was even a diamond necklace for Roz, apparently a family heirloom. I don't know. That Christening gown was designed by—"

"Yeah, people have money," Luca said, "but so did you, and *do* … with us. I guess."

"No, it's not *that* … I just meant, my gift doesn't really compare. To either the cost or the thoughtfulness and I—"

"Roz doesn't care about that shit. What is it?"

Penny's stare pleaded for him to stop talking.

Luca wouldn't.

"Seriously, what did you get her? Or make … you said both, right?"

"I mean, yeah, but—"

"Don't be silly."

"Don't call me *silly*." Penny glared.

*Whoa.*

The sharpness in her tone, like the idea of him thinking she was childish, was enough to earn that kind of reaction from her, had him blinking for a second. Luca played it off, though.

"Just…" Luca nodded at the gift, saying when he smiled, "What is it?"

"A teddy bear. When you press the hand, it plays a song I composed and recorded. I know it's not … nothing, but it doesn't feel like *something*, either."

That took Luca a minute.

"As in a song you composed recently?" he asked.

Because he knew … Roz had said many times, and so did Naz in passing, that Penny had shown very little interest in returning to the piano since coming to live with them. And if she had spent the time composing, playing, and recording a song for his sister's unborn baby, that would be huge. A gift that couldn't *be* compared considering everything.

"Yeah, I made it just for the baby."

*Oh.*

Luca stared at the empty hallway behind Penny, shaking his head. "Give her the gift, Penny. It'll mean … everything to Roz. Even if you do it privately, I promise she will love it."

*Beyond*, even.

"You think?" Penny asked, glancing up at him with worry in wide eyes.

"I know."

"Okay." Penny hugged the gift closer, then, saying, "Thanks."

Luca stepped aside in the hallway to let Penny passing, replying easily, "No problem. That's what friends do for each other. It's okay to need that sometimes—a friend, you know?"

She hesitated in her next step, those clear blue eyes of hers nailing to his when she asked, "Is that what you are to me—a friend?"

"Yeah, I can be your friend, Penny."

"Never really had one of those."

Luca smiled. "I'm happy to be your first."

# *15.*

*Penny*

IT was almost strange how fast things could change. One minute, Penny had finally gained the courage to give Roz her gift, and the next … Baby Cross was on his way. Roz went into labor while Penny sat beside her.

Or, her water broke.

The labor pain came after.

Everyone was so *calmly* excited when Penny had found Naz inside the party and delivered the news.

"You were right, by the way," Penny said.

To her companion who was currently sitting in the hard, waiting room chair beside hers. There wasn't anything comfortable about the seats, and even then as she could barely stand to keep her eyes open for another minute, she used Luca's side to lean against as some form of cushion.

Which wasn't much.

He was also hard—just in a different way. She didn't mind his hard warmth nearly as much as the cold plastic of the chair, though.

"About?" she heard Luca ask, his voice a murmur.

The exhaustion was clear in his tone. Like hers, too.

What time was it?

Penny didn't know.

She also didn't care to ask anyone else waiting there with them. That would mean speaking to people, and she wasn't really in the mood when all she wanted to do was have a little nap. Once she realized—after Roz was admitted to a room where they were only allowed two support people to stay during birth—that it was going to be hours before the baby boy actually made his appearance, she asked Luca to take her home.

Not because she didn't want to stay.

No, Penny remembered the dishes in the sink that Roz had left to load in the dishwasher before they left for the party. After she cleaned that, Luca helped to fix up the bathroom that the girls had used to ready for the party. And the explosion of clothes and everything else on the bed in Roz and Naz's room. The laundry that had been left in the washer and dryer downstairs came next.

They also traveled two loads of gifts back to the house so then Naz and Roz wouldn't have to worry about any of that when the time came. Once the house was in a better state—not that it was dirty in the first place—the two did a mop and sweep of the floors just because. It was one less thing for Naz or Roz to do when they arrived home, right?

That's what she thought.

Luca didn't mind.

Now that the two of them were finally back at the hospital, though, she was *tired*. She hadn't even bothered to change out of the black dress that Roz convinced her to wear for the party. The item, at first, only made her cringe away. It was too tight—form-fitted in every possible way. She also needed flesh-colored tights underneath because it stopped at her knees. It was the first time she wore heels in … *years*.

Yet, when she pulled the dress on, something was *right*. Maybe it was the way she could admire how her waist looked cinched in the middle or how her hips and breasts curved to give her that hourglass appearance. Somehow, in the many years that Penny had spent hiding her body, she missed when it grew into something different.

A young woman's form.

Soft curves.

She still remembered thinking that she looked fragile in some ways. Unsure, even, as she took in the changes that could come to her own body—and even in her mind—simply by putting on a dress. It was frightening.

And yet, she liked it, too.

She *liked* the way she looked.

That was just …

It blew her mind.

"Penny?" Luca asked.

She felt him lean forward like he was checking to see if she had fallen asleep leaning against him when she remained silent.

"Sorry, I was thinking," she replied.

"About me being right?"

Ah, yeah.

She forgot about that.

"No, other things." Sighing, Penny shifted a bit on the chair to lift her feet and set them on the other seat. It helped with the tension in her back, anyway. "You were right about giving Roz the gift and not being worried."

She swore she could hear Luca's smile behind her when he replied, "She loved it."

It wasn't even a question.

"Yeah, she did," Penny whispered.

Maybe a part of her knew Roz would appreciate the simple bear with his beautiful song—a lullaby Penny composed for the baby. She'd stressed so much leading up to actually figuring out what she wanted to get Roz for her shower that when she did sit down and record the song, it came painfully easy. She just … thought about how scary everything was for her sometimes. It couldn't be that much different to a new baby meeting the world for the first time.

So, the song needed to be soothing. Soft notes that carried from one verse to the next. A tune that could be listened to without it becoming overwhelming. Something that would lull a baby into … *comfort.*

She wanted to comfort little Cross when he was new and scared. The notes came easier when she thought of it that way. Hopefully, because she really wanted to, she would be able to play it for the baby herself while she held him.

Wouldn't that be nice?

"Told you," Luca said.

He didn't even sound smug about it.

At least, there was that.

"A lot has changed," Penny said.

"Hmm—like what?"

"Me."

That quieted Luca.

Penny didn't mind.

Even when she took the time to think about everything that was different in her life now—since moving in with Naz and Roz—it was enough to draw her into silence. The heavy kind that sometimes came with dull aches deep in her heart and things she wasn't always willing to face. She still did, though.

Didn't that count for something?

God.

She hoped so.

Penny was still trying.

It's all they asked.

"Have you changed, or your circumstances?" Luca asked.

Well …

"Both," she replied.

Months ago, she never would have cared that her graduation was just weeks away. Baby Cross would still be brand new when she walked across the stage. Back then, she wasn't counting down the days until she turned eighteen—a few more months.

She had new musical pursuits on the table if she wanted to make the attempt. She was going to be a godmother.

Lately, she didn't focus on the things that had happened leading up to all of this … change. She found it was easier to leave the memories of her father and mother behind. Or as much as she could, anyway.

It wasn't perfect.

Life was certainly different.

"But I like it," she told Luca.

Like the dress.

Her changes.

*Everything.*

When she shivered in the chair, because waiting rooms weren't known for their heat, Luca shifted again before the leather jacket he'd grabbed out of his car earlier suddenly dropped down on top of her. He made quick work of shifting it around so that it covered Penny like a blanket. All the while, he said nothing.

He didn't need to.

Now, he was all around her.

Support behind her.

Warmth she needed.

*More.*

Every breath she took brought with it the smell of him that clung to the leather jacket. The barest hints of cigarette smoke—she never saw him smoke—mixed in with something crisp, like pine needles, and the leather of the jacket.

"Is it scary?" Luca asked.

Penny was almost asleep now. "What?"

"When things change."

"Yes," she replied simply.

Because it was.

When everything was good, she found herself worrying about what was going to go wrong. Not that she dared to say it out loud. Then, it might actually happen.

"Luca?"

"Hmm?" he asked.

In her state—almost asleep but still partly awake—Penny wasn't even sure if the conversation she was having was real or just something she was manifesting. Even so, she kept talking, telling Luca, "I liked you at first because of the way you looked."

It took her a while to accept that fact, really. It wasn't an easy conclusion to come to because she didn't like the idea of being attracted to someone for the sake of attraction. Hadn't she learned long ago that just because something *looked* pretty didn't mean it actually was?

Luca proved her wrong.

*Again.*

A muffled chuckle answered her back. "Oh?"

"Yeah."

But … *look at him.* A single look from him screamed with intensity that Penny really didn't know how to deal with. Especially when she knew his stares often accompanied his kindness and wisdom. He didn't stare to …

appraise her. He did it to find who she was.

Who wouldn't notice a face like Luca's first?

"But then I liked you because you were kind and helpful," Penny added as the darkness shrouded her vision, and she smiled. "And because you made me talk—you weren't scared of me like everyone else is. You cared."

And she just thought he should know.

"Go to sleep, Penny."

She sighed. "Okay."

• • •

"Don't hide over there," Roz told Penny.

Standing in the doorway of the bedroom, Penny didn't dare step any closer to Roz and the bundle of blue she held in the rocking chair. "What if I wake him up?"

"He's sleeping. *Happily*. He just ate. Milk drunk."

What?

Penny giggled but quickly slapped a hand over her mouth to hush the noise. "Sorry."

Roz rolled her eyes and gave Penny a look. For just having a baby, and being home only a day, she thought Roz looked … *great*. Glowing, even. She hadn't done much with her dark hair but throw it up in a messy bun. She was even wearing one of those tracksuits she had previously told Penny was only good for being lazy.

And yet, she was beautiful.

Full of pride.

And happiness.

Like a new mother should be.

"You're *not* going to wake him up," Roz assured. "And besides, we don't want everyone tiptoeing around every time he lays down to sleep. He'll never learn to sleep through the noise that way. Just come here."

Penny did.

Still hesitant, though.

At Roz's side, she looked down to find the baby *was* sleeping and perfectly content wrapped in a blue blanket while he was rocked in his mother's arm. He sucked on the side of his hand while black tufts of hair peeked out from beneath his wool cap.

It wasn't even the tenth time Penny laid eyes on baby Cross since he was born and yet … it still felt like it. Each time she stared down at his small features, she easily found his father and how much he took after Nazio. She found the peacefulness of a baby in his gassy grins and hazy eyes—when they were open, of course.

She found someone she loved.

"Roz?"

Both Penny and Roz glanced toward the doorway at the new voice. Naz grinned in at them, and then said, "Your mom and dad just got here. Do you want to come down for a minute? They said to let the little guy sleep for now."

"I'll be down in a sec."

"All right, babe."

After Naz disappeared, Roz turned to Penny, asking, "Do you want to rock him for a little while? If you want after you can just put him in his bassinet."

Penny didn't even think about it. "Sure."

Before long, it was just Penny and the baby boy alone in the master bedroom. She wasn't sure how long she sat rocking a sleeping Cross while she stared down at his face, imprinting every little thing about him to her memory, but it didn't matter. There was nothing else she wanted to do more than be right there.

Staring at him.

He was kind of perfect.

Helpless.

*Innocent.*

The only things he wanted from the world—at the moment, anyway—was his mother, milk, and warmth when he slept. Everything else that he *needed* … well, he didn't know about those things. He didn't know that rocking him made him fall asleep faster. Or that he was tiny and needed a whole house to keep him safe. Those were the things the rest of them did for him whether he knew it or not.

Penny didn't mind at all.

What was he going to be like?

How would he grow?

She could only imagine who little Cross would be as he became older, started to walk and talk, and went from a baby to a toddling boy. It wasn't lost on Penny how she felt such an instant familial connection to the baby when she barely felt anything for people who were her actual family.

Blood meant nothing.

She understood that now.

There was also something else that kept prickling at the back of Penny's mind every time she held the baby. This would never be her—a woman holding her own child; one she birthed. She was too young for kids, anyway, but it wouldn't happen for her in the future, either.

Not that she had dared to tell anyone else because the heavy sadness wasn't really something she could explain without also needing to say *why*. She didn't want to get into all that.

"Roz said you were up here. How's he doing?"

Penny's head snapped up, and her gaze found Luca leaning in the doorway. "I didn't know you were—"

"Came with Ma and Dad."

Oh.

Penny smiled down at the baby. "He's great."

"I bet. You look happy."

Did she?

Penny nodded. "I am. But also a little sad."

Of course, Luca would ask, "Why?"

He always asked questions. Even when she didn't want to answer.

"It doesn't matter," Penny said.

She hoped he leave it alone.

He didn't.

*Surprise.*

Luca's footsteps approached until he was standing beside the rocking chair and looking down on the two. Reaching over, he pulled back the blanket a little more from baby Cross's cheek to expose the hand he was sucking on.

"I think everything matters," Luca replied quietly. "But especially the things you think *don't*."

Well …

What would it hurt to tell one person? Another secret clawed at Penny.

It wanted out.

"Friends keep secrets, right?" she asked.

Luca chuckled under his breath. "They do."

"I can't have my own kids. I never really thought that I wanted them anyway, but I guess when you hold a baby … you think about it more. What it might be like, you know?"

"What?"

Penny refused to look up at Luca, instead keeping her attention focused on the bundle in her arms. "It's not a big deal—"

"It's a *huge* deal."

Maybe to him.

She had always known.

Or at least since …

"I was given a tubal ligation when I was ten—before my period even started. In my records, and what I was told at the time, was that I was having surgery for appendicitis. Except I heard my parents talking. And the doctor they paid off to do it. So, I'll … never have my own. And maybe I just realized that I might want to."

Penny hadn't expected a response.

How did one respond to that?

Luca still surprised her.

He always did.

A tight hug that felt like *safety* found her as his warmth and scent wrapped all around her. One traitorous tear slipped out of the corner of her eye when she heard him murmur against the top of her head, "I'm sorry, Penny."

Who knew?

Who knew an apology—even if this man had nothing to apologize to her for—could feel like healing? Sometimes, it was all she needed, though.

For someone …

*Anyone* to say sorry.

And fucking mean it.

She just wanted people to mean it.

# 16.

*Penny*

FOR once, when the months passed without Penny really noticing, it wasn't because she was depressed. The months leading up to her eighteenth birthday saw her graduate high school—a feat in itself. She never expected to walk across that stage and feel a sense of accomplishment simply for doing it.

But she did.

On the way to turning eighteen, she also got to watch baby Cross go from a sleepy newborn to a constantly babbling, sweet six-month-old. Maybe that was what made the months go by so fast. Before she had even blinked, really. She heard everyone tell Roz—over and over—to enjoy the time she had with her son as a baby because soon, it would change. *Babies don't stay babies for long.*

Those people were right.

*Mostly.*

Penny *wanted* to see little Cross grow. She looked forward to getting up every day just to see what the baby was going to do that day. It seemed like he did something new every time. She was lucky enough to watch him do it, too.

Turning eighteen meant a lot of things to Penny. It always had even long before she came to stay with Naz and Roz. Eighteen felt like freedom. Of sorts. Freedom over herself, if she wanted, when she finally became an actual legal adult under the law. An adult capable of making her own decisions, living where—and as—she wanted, and even … leaving.

Because a long time ago, all she thought about was leaving. Back when she was being abused and trafficked by her father, or even after when she was shuffled from one private school to another to keep her issues a secret from anyone that cared enough to try to help, leaving was the one thing she held onto. Or rather, turning eighteen so she *could* leave.

But then it happened.

Eighteen came and went.

What did Penny do?

She stayed. Right where she was, actually. Roz asked once if Penny wanted to look at apartments in the city—as she had been offered a spot as the lead pianist in a famous Manhattan company when someone pulled a few strings—but she said no. How was she going to still manage to see her godson every day being there?

At least now, she got to wake up to him. And if she did take the spot in the company, she would still wake up to the boy and then head back to home at night where he was waiting for her.

"Are you okay?"

Penny had been so lost in her thoughts that she didn't even realize the elevator they were riding to a higher floor of an attorney's office had come to a stop. While Roz stood beside her holding baby Cross against her hip, Luca was at the elevator doors holding it open and looking their way. He had come along for the day trip to the office in place of Naz, who was busy.

What was today?

Oh, just another great part of turning eighteen.

*Great*, right.

Penny was finally getting her trust fund signed over. Along with the restitution payments from her deceased father's estate. She didn't actually want any of it, but that wasn't her choice. As she had been told many times over, what she did with the money after the accounts were in her name wasn't their business, but it did have to be *hers*.

For a time, anyway.

"Penny?" Roz asked.

Penny looked Roz's way, seeing the worry staring back at her. Shit, even *she* was worried. She hadn't been this quiet in months. She had, after all, learned how to have conversations with other people and enjoy it. She didn't need to be lost inside her head all the time now.

"I don't want to be here," Penny admitted.

"I know," Roz replied, "but it won't be for long. You'll sign some papers, get the information you need, and once everything is good, we're gone."

"Just like that," Luca added, drawing Penny's attention his way, too. "No worries."

Easy for them to say.

They weren't facing a meeting with their horrible, manipulative mot—

"Ah, there you are!" A familiar man in a suit—one of the lawyers on Penny's side of things, stepped out of a room down the hallway from the elevator and headed their way. "We were waiting for you before starting. The other beneficiary to the estate asked for us to do so. Are you about ready?"

All eyes turned on Penny.

That other beneficiary to her father's estate?

It was Penny's mother.

And no.

She was nowhere near ready.

• • •

Nearly two years had passed since Penny laid eyes on Allegra Dunsworth. Even before she became a ward of the state and her mother signed away any legal right to her own child, there had been entire seas and continents between them for … a long time.

The last thing her mother said to her?

Penny could still remember it like it was yesterday.

*"It's not okay," she told her mother. "It's not."*

*Allegra only shook her head. "You don't even understand what I've given you—you're not worthy."*

For most of her youth, Penny had been far too young to understand that the sexual abuse she suffered under her father—but with her mother's permission, encouragement, and even *control*—was bigger than just what it appeared to be on the surface. The blackened veins of abuse had begun long before Penny was even a thought in her parents' marriage. Before her mother was even married to begin with, honestly.

It started with Allegra and her own father, but even that wasn't the first in their family's legacy. It was simply something her mother continued on, while her father pulled the strings from the shadows, growing their disgusting inclinations and dark family secrets into a terrifyingly successful organization where cash was king. And the young princes and princesses were broken on the piles of dirty money.

Absolute power corrupts absolutely.

Wasn't that how the saying went?

Allegra and her father weren't the only people with attractions that society said wasn't *acceptable*. But money could do anything—it made everyone talk and walk.

Penny learned too young—but also too late—what it meant to be a Dunsworth girl. A pretty, compliant, *good* Dunsworth girl.

And when she finally gained the courage to tell her mother as a broken teenage girl, that what they did to her wasn't okay … Allegra replied that she wasn't worthy.

Worthy of what?

Clawing depression?

The constant shame?

Knowing what they were doing to others even if she was no longer *useable*?

That was the last time she spoke or saw her mother in almost two years. Now, sitting on the other side of a long table with lawyers all around them, Penny and Luca on either side of her, and even baby Cross in his mother's lap babbling on with preciousness like he always did … the only thing she could see was Allegra.

At the other side.

Staring her down.

Smiling *so* sweetly.

She heard them talking.

Lawyers doing their … thing.

Roz telling her, "Nearly done, Penny."

Even Luca telling his godson, "Nah, buddy—we don't eat the paper. That shit's trash."

She looked just like her mother.

They were also totally different.

Allegra in her white dress, a capped sleeve number that plunged in the front while her white-blonde hair had been let down in soft curves over her shoulders. Penny had opted for skinny jeans and a loose blouse that she let Roz convince her to at least try the last time they went shopping.

During their final conversation, and even before that, Allegra had never seen Penny in anything but clothes she could practically swim in. Her naked body hadn't been displayed in front of her mother—in the flesh—since she was twelve. Yet, with a table between them, and clothes she knew covered her body, though not comfortable enough to hide her shape—she could feel Allegra's gaze appraising her.

That was what her mother had meant.

Her *worth* was always one thing.

"Okay, I'm just gonna run down the hall to the quiet room and feed him really quickly," Roz said, finally dragging Penny's stunned attention away from her mother. "And I think someone needs a diaper—*fuck*."

All the lawyers quieted at the cuss.

Roz's cheeks pinked when she muttered to Luca, "I forgot the diaper bag in the car. Naz always grabs it, I wasn't even thinking and didn't mention to you to grab it."

"I can get it."

"But Penny—"

Their gazes darted to her instantly.

Penny wanted to ask them not to go. Her heart *screamed* it. Yet, the fear was so overwhelming; the absolute terror of being this close to her mother had been enough of a shock to her system that she had shut down a while ago.

Back when they first entered the room.

"You okay for us to go?" Luca asked. "I'll be back in a few minutes. The lawyers are all here. Right?"

Her shoulders lifted—something akin to a shrug—but it was all she could manage. Luca and Roz took that as an okay.

See, she'd never been honest.

Not completely.

Penny's biggest demon wasn't a man long dead. The monster hiding in the depths of her soul wasn't every man who had ever used her body as a child for their sexual pleasure. The truth was far more frightening than that. *Who* haunted her was more real than all of that combined.

She had the chance to take them down.

And currently … Allegra was still smiling at her.

Like Penny should already know what would happen next.

Maybe she did.

• • •

Penny's fear got ahead of itself … *thankfully*. She hadn't even needed to speak to her mother—or barely look at the woman—once the lawyers really got down to business. Allegra had her side of things, the estate had its own lawyers, and then Penny had hers as well. Signing her signature on all the *many* dotted lines ended up taking the bulk of the time. Luca ended up being back in lots of time while Roz remained in the quiet room feeding the baby.

Once it was all said and done, Penny was shuffled out of the room by her lawyers, given a folder and told, "That's it. And when—or if—you want access to the money, you walk into the bank and tell them what to do with it."

That was it.

"Everything good?" Roz asked when Penny came to stand in the doorway of the quiet room. "I'm almost done."

The shawl Roz had thrown around her son while he drank his bottle did little to hide his wiggling feet. It was cute. Something he had always done, even when he was brand new, while someone fed the boy.

"Yeah, it looks like we're finished with our side of things," Luca said for Penny. "The estate lawyer is in there with the other one, but that doesn't involve us. So, whenever you're done we can leave. I'm gonna go use the bathroom before we go."

"All right," Roz replied to her brother.

Luca headed down the hallway near the bank of elevators where a sign pointed around a corner for the bathrooms.

Penny let out a little sigh. "That went easier than I thought it would."

"Of course, it did. Just some paperwork."

Right.

Well, that's what she wanted Roz to think. There was no reason to worry her with things that hadn't even happened—like a confrontation with her mother.

While Roz went back to feeding the baby, Penny lingered out in the hallway just beyond the visibility of the doorway to the quiet room. She wanted a minute alone—even if it was only a *sense* of privacy in some way—to hold the weight of the folder in her hands that now said she was the recipient of several of her father's millions.

She still hadn't figured out what to do with it or—

"Will you look at me now?"

Penny's head snapped up at the quiet question. Somehow, in her distraction, she had missed Allegra leaving the conference room to come and stand in the hallway. Just ten feet away from Penny. Ten short steps separated her from the person who had caused her the most pain.

And probably wasn't done, she knew. Because that was the thing about her mother … it never really felt *over.*

"I—"

"You do know why I allowed you to leave the country the first time, don't you? Why I kept you in private schools?" her mother asked.

Penny swallowed hard. "It fixed a problem."

"In a sense. I gave you what you wanted—to be away from it all—and it corrected the issue of having you near. Coming back wasn't any different, was it?"

*What?*

"Penny," Allegra said, her voice still soft and musical, enough to draw even the most guarded souls close, "you didn't talk—so I signed you away. You got something you wanted, and so did I. Fixing another problem."

Right, right.

"Except it isn't enough," her mother said, drawing Penny's gaze upward until the two were staring at one another. The memories of a time long gone rushed past Penny's eyes, moments that had never truly left her mind despite hiding as well as they had for all this time. Cement might as well have been poured into her feet as Allegra took those ten steps between them and turned it into only a foot. She could smell the peony perfume her mother had always worn. "I know who they are, Penny."

"Who—"

"The people you're with now. I know *who* they are, what they do, and even what they *can* do. And if they try to come after me, or anyone near me, for you … if I even feel a little bit threatened by any Donati, I'll burn them to the ground. And you know I won't care if you burn with them."

Panic swelled in her heart.

It *hurt.*

She didn't want Allegra anywhere near Roz, Naz, the baby … *anyone* she loved. None of them.

"They don't know any—"

"Yet, but," Allegra replied, "I'll be watching you. All of you."

Penny took a step back from her mother at the same time a new voice from behind her said, "Everything okay out here?"

*Roz.*

Penny turned to tell Roz to back into the quiet room, but Allegra's smile was all she could see as the woman passed her by to come closer. She reached out a single hand, each finger adorned by a thin golden ring, for the baby. Like she was going to touch baby Cross's hand.

The baby pulled away, dark eyes narrowed and brow furrowed on the stranger in front of him. Except he looked at her like … he recognized her. Or something about her.

Something bad.

Except that was impossible.

He was just a baby.

"He's adorable," Allegra told Roz. "He must be what, six months? I always wanted a boy … and thank you for taking care of Penny. I was never a very good mother. I hoped she found someone who could give her what I couldn't. Seems that was you, hmm?"

That was it.

Allegra offered one more smile and then turned on her heel and past Penny. The two shared a look—nothing that visually threatening, but it didn't have to be, either.

Penny said nothing.

She couldn't.

"Did she know?" Roz asked as Allegra slipped down the hall and Penny's heart shattered into a million and one pieces all around her.

"Know—what do you mean?"

Oh, good.

There was her voice again.

At least, she hadn't lost it forever.

"Sorry," Roz muttered, obviously hearing the pain in Penny's tone. "I've never asked about … the things your father did to you. I never wanted to push. It's none of my business. You can forget I even asked if you want. I just … wondered for a second."

*Ah.*

Penny understood. "You meant … did she know my father was sexually abusing me and selling me to other men to do the same while it was happening?"

Roz let out a hard breath. "Yeah, see, when you lay it all out like that—it's a harder pill to swallow than the way I make myself think about it, Penny."

Honesty was a killer.

But … "That was my life, though."

"And I'm so sorry."

"I know, Roz. I *do*."

"But it doesn't help, does it."

Well, that was the thing about it.

Penny smiled faintly, whispering, "It does help."

Baby Cross reached for her, and she held his tiny hand with three fingers that he tried to pull into his drool-filled mouth.

"It helps to have people who really love me," she added, not looking Roz in the eye. "Because you mean it—you really *are* sorry for the things that happened to me even if you weren't a cause or able to stop it. For the first time ever, I didn't feel crazy, Roz. When I felt *bad* ... when I knew things weren't right, I was told I was wrong. It's the people who love me and tell me they're sorry for what others did to me that taught me I wasn't wrong at all. In a lot of ways."

"Oh, Penny—"

"Do you really want to know?" she asked Roz, swallowing hard. "If she knew ... the *truth*?"

Unshed tears filled Roz's eyes when Penny met her gaze. "You told me once ... one of the first times we met, actually, that if you opened your mouth and started talking about everything, nothing would be the same, right?"

"But I only talked a little."

"Enough to put your father in prison," Roz returned.

"Enough to be *free*. Do you want the truth?" Penny asked again.

Roz blinked, the tears falling when she whispered, "I do."

"She always knew."

The silence came without mercy.

Roz held a little tighter to her infant son, glancing down the hall where Allegra had disappeared to return to her lawyers. "Sh-she smiled and seemed purposefully *nice* and—something felt wrong about it. He wouldn't let her touch his hand. Did you see that?"

Baby Cross was back to babbling and smacking the side of his hand against his mouth. A typical baby. But for a second, *yes*, Penny had seen the way the baby pulled *away* from her mother. Like a part of him instinctually knew she was all wrong.

The same way Penny knew.

Just like Roz said it all felt *wrong*.

"Are we ready or what?" Luca asked, breaking Penny and Roz's locked gazes as he came around the corner of the hallway with dripping wet hands. "Ignore the water—they only had blow dryers, and everybody knows that shit spreads *everything*. They'll airdry. Are we ready to go now, or *what*?"

"Yeah," Roz said, "we're ready. Let's go."

Penny was happy to follow along, only wanting to get as far away from her mother as she possibly could. At the same time, all she could think about was her mother's parting words to her.

*I'll be watching you. All of you.*

Allegra's threats against Penny and anyone close to her weren't empty. But what could she do now?

How could Penny protect anyone? She hadn't even been able to protect herself.

• • •

Penny let Naz and Roz throw a party. For her eighteenth birthday, that was.

She wished she hadn't.

If only she could have foreseen the way a single conversation with her mother could send Penny flying back in *so many ways* … Her nightmares were back. She could barely breathe when someone stood too close to her. Every room was too small to be inside for any length of time, but the outside was even more terrifying.

Nothing was right.

Everything was entirely *wrong*.

Just like her mother.

Roz brushed off Penny's snappiness and quiet demeanor as stress leading up to the massive eighteenth birthday party. She even told the teenager that she would be more surprised if Penny *wasn't* in a mood lately.

That only made her feel worse.

The guilt was a killer.

Still, she couldn't tell the truth.

Didn't dare.

What if her mother—

Penny slammed the heavy door of the mansion's library closed behind her, dragging in a breath that shook and ached the whole way in. Her palms pressed against the wood as she listened to the hum of the party and music down the hall while she tried to soothe the panic attack clawing its way through her nervous system.

*Too many people.*

*Too many smiles.*

*Too many lies.*

Because she was putting them all in danger—every single one of them. Just by being there. What happened if her mother changed her mind … what if just telling wasn't a good enough reason for Allegra—and all the people connected to her mother's business—to kill Penny?

She sucked in a ragged breath, letting go of the door to wipe the wet tears that had fallen in her haste to get away from the party before anyone could even notice she was gone. No doubt, someone would come looking for her soon.

Wasn't that the entire point?

This was supposed to be her night.

*Her* eighteenth birthday party.

Fuck.

It was something she *wanted.* For the first time, she wanted to be celebrated. Why did her mother have to ruin something else that should have been *just* for Penny?

"I'm not equipped to deal with the tears of a teenage girl—should I leave?"

The new—*male*—voice had Penny swinging around on the spot. The library doors pressed against her back as she found a familiar man watching her from the other side of the room. Behind the large desk in the library, he stood drinking what looked to be whiskey on ice as he observed her mental breakdown with nothing more than a cocked eyebrow. His eyes were dark—soul-deep, some might say, but cold, too.

In the time she had been with Naz and Roz, she could count on one hand the number of conversations she had had with the man staring at her.

Cross Donati, that was.

Naz's father.

*Head of the family*, she knew.

It was never said.

Just … understood.

"I could get my wife," he suggested, tipping his glass her way when more tears spilled down Penny's cheeks. "Or even Roz, if you want. I mean, it's your call but—"

"It's fine," she rushed to say.

She didn't want *anyone* to know something was wrong. Not when she wasn't sure what that might mean for them to know in the first place. Or worse … because she did know exactly what it would mean.

Her reply had Cross narrowing his gaze on her. "You're lying."

"What?"

"You're lying to me. I don't know why, maybe it's not important. But you *are* lying, and that's … interesting."

"Wh-why?" she asked, more confused than anything.

"Because that means something really is wrong. But if it was the kind of something Roz could handle, and she usually does with you, I know that for a fact, then you wouldn't have just refused my offer to get her. So, something is wrong … and it's bad, isn't it?"

Penny swallowed hard, unsettled with how the man had been able to read her without any effort at all. That was a gift most people didn't possess—she also didn't know what to do about it.

Except stay silent.

"Penny—"

"It's fine," she said again.

*Nope.*

It didn't work.

He rounded the desk, taking slow, short steps until he stopped in the middle of the room. "You were doing well—Naz said so. He did mention you've been a little off for about a week. Since what, the day your trust and restitution was handed over, right?"

She didn't reply.

He didn't need her to, apparently.

"I heard your mother was there," he said.

Cross stared at her like he *knew* … but what?

How could he?

*Who was he if he did know?*

"No Roz, then?" he asked quietly.

Penny nodded. "Please."

"Okay. Is it bad? Whatever happened … is it bad?"

"Yeah."

"Do you need help?"

"Everyone does," Penny admitted. "They all need help because of me."

He dragged in a heavy breath and scrubbed his hand back through the slick strands of his dark hair, peppered with gray only at the edges. "Then, tell me. Can't I help?"

She hesitated. Only for a second. Then she thought … *what do I have to lose now?* The answer was scary.

*Everything.*

Penny whispered to the man still looking her way, "They call themselves, The Elite."

And she told him all of it.

Every sordid detail she knew.

# 17.

*Luca*

FOR once, Luca hadn't been late to a party. He was starting to think his family and friends might withhold invitations—joking, of course.

Naz slapped Luca on the shoulder as the two of them faced the large rose gold three-tier cake with the sparkling *18* resting at the very top proudly. "Didn't think we were going to make it to this point if I'm being honest. It's not a bad thing for me to want to … celebrate that as a personal accomplishment, is it?"

Luca grinned his friend's way, knowing the truth. Naz and Roz had nothing but goodness in their hearts where Penny was concerned. So … "Yeah, I think you earned a bit of celebrating."

"Me, too, man."

Turning back around to face the rest of the room, they surveyed the people milling between the grand rooms of the Donati mansion. Another party that everyone decided was better thrown at someone else's house because of space. Given the number of people who showed up to support Penny's birthday party, he had to admit the suggestion wasn't a bad one. There had to be at least a hundred people.

Or more.

He found his parents in the crowd standing next to Naz's. *As usual.* His sister drifted between guests with a smile on her face, talking to everyone like she did because that was just Roz in a nutshell. Servers from the company his family liked to use for larger events—when the ladies couldn't handle making all the food themselves—kept everyone's hands full with either treats or something to drink.

The party was in full swing.

Had been for a while.

And that's when Luca realized he needed to ask, "Where's Penny?"

He was sure he'd gotten a peek of her earlier talking to Naz's grandmother, Emma, but it was brief before he was pulled away. Shit, he hadn't even been able to tell her happy birthday—even if he did tell her the day she actually turned eighteen.

"I don't know," Naz said, sucking hair through his teeth. "Fuck, I wonder if she found somewhere to hide for a bit. There's a lot of people here. We told her it was okay if—"

"Want me to find her?"

Naz laughed. "Would you?"

"Yeah, why not?"

It wasn't like he was doing anything but standing there. At least this way, Luca would *look* busy. Maybe then his father would quit shooting looks his way like Zeke was going to come over and find something new to run his mouth about.

But who could say?

Certainly not Luca.

"I'll find her," he promised his friend.

At his back, Naz called, "But don't make her do shit if she's not in the mood. We're still surprised she even let us do this."

That was fair.

Luca was surprised, too.

It took him longer to find Penny in the mansion than he cared to admit. She wasn't anywhere that he thought she would be. Certainly not mingling with the people or sneaking sweets from the kitchen where the caterers had been set up. He even checked in the rear of the mansion to see if she might have slipped outside for a breather.

No such luck.

It was on his way back from checking outside that he finally found her. At first, though, he didn't even realize it *was* Penny. The royal blue skirt of her dress fell over her hips and the pert roundness of her backside in such a way that he couldn't help himself but stare when she bent over the side of an infant's Pack 'n Play to rest baby Cross at the bottom.

The baby was already sleeping, from what he could see of the still infant at the bottom of the bed. And Luca was still staring at *Penny's* ass when she leaned further down to kiss the baby boy on his forehead.

It took him entirely too long to realize it *was* Penny. That was half the problem. In just a short couple of months, a lot about Penny had started to change. She tried more things—*new* things that he didn't expect her to. Like makeup and clothes more suited to a young woman. She still liked an oversized hoodie every once in a while, but at least now, someone could actually see that she did have a shape under all those layers of clothes.

He just wished *he* didn't notice.

Luca didn't need that problem. He refused to even admire the fact that the dress, the matte, flesh-toned stockings, and the matching blue, pointed-toed heels made her calves look fucking perfect.

*Too late, stupid.*

He shook those thoughts off. And the indecent feelings.

She was only eighteen. Still *way* too damn young for him and *hell* … Luca hadn't even seen Penny in that kind of way before. He wasn't about to start now. It wasn't happening.

*Nope.*

Stepping back out of view of the doorway, he waited for Penny to finish her business in the baby's makeshift bedroom for the night. At least, it gave him a few extra minutes to get out of that crazy fucking headspace.

One good thing.

There wasn't much else.

He hadn't expected Penny to be wiping away tears when she stepped out of the room and closed the door behind her. To be fair, she hadn't expected him to be standing there waiting for her, either, if the way she jumped and swallowed a half-shriek into the palm she slapped over her mouth was any indication.

"Sorry," Luca said. "Naz wanted me to find you. I guess you disappeared. You okay?"

Penny shrugged and played with the long sleeves of the royal blue dress that dipped low at her chest with a cut V neckline. The skirt swished from side to side where it fell a few inches below her knees when she shifted from heel to heel. "Yeah, I'm okay."

"Tears don't usually mean *okay*, Penny."

She rolled sparkling blue eyes.

*Oh, now they sparkle.*

Luca ignored his taunting inner thoughts.

Fucking prick.

"I'm fine," she said, peeking back at the door she had closed. "Just saying goodbye."

"Goodnight, you mean?"

Because goodbye implied—

"Yeah, goodnight," Penny rushed to say, laughing at her mistake. He still thought it sounded … *wrong*. Fake, maybe. "Tonight has me all messed up. Too many people, you know?"

Luca grinned. "Yeah, I know. They're over the moon that you let them do this, though. For the record."

"I know. I do."

"You wanna head back to the party or do you need a few more minutes?"

Penny turned her smile on him, and for a second, he just *blinked*. The soft, natural tones of her makeup really set off the shape of her face while her white-blonde hair had been left down in soft waves to frame her features and fall over her shoulders. She might have been only eighteen, but he was *not* blind.

She was stunning.

*Finally* shedding her shell.

Luca thought she deserved to know. "You look beautiful, by the way. Who picked the dress?"

Penny beamed even through the pink blush that colored her cheeks and rushed down the exposed part of her chest. She didn't meet his gaze when she replied, "Me, but Roz convinced me to wear it when I second-guessed it today."

*Ah.*

Good going, Roz.

He didn't say that out loud.

*Barely.*

"The shoes kind of hurt," she added.

Both of them looked down at the pointed toe, blue heels.

"Shame, they make your legs look fantastic."

*Fuck.*

Penny's head lifted slowly, her gaze finally finding his, but he did his best to stare down the hall and pretend like that thought hadn't slipped out of his mouth. His incredibly *stupid* mouth. Such was his luck, Penny hadn't missed it anyway.

"Luca—"

"It shouldn't be *me*," he muttered, his stare snapping back to hold hers strong while he spoke. "You shouldn't break your teeth in on me while you figure out what you want with men or *sex* … whatever, even if I could handle it. I said I was gonna be your friend, Penny. A safe place, right? And I'm not sure I can be that if there isn't a line."

*There.*

He said it.

The truth was out there.

"Okay," she whispered.

He couldn't even pretend like he was incapable of seeing the line of water in her bright eyes. She did her very best to keep them from falling when she blinked them away, though.

"And I'm sorry," he added, clearing the thickness from his throat.

Penny's brow lifted when she asked, "For *what?*"

"I'm a shitty friend, anyway. I didn't get you anything for your birthday."

He was still running like a madman for Naz and trying to keep up with college, after all. He was lucky that he even made it to this goddamn party on time. Accomplishing anything in his life currently felt like a feat. When would that change?

"You're my best friend, actually," Penny replied, smiling softly with painted pink lips. "My first *real* friend. And I think that's a good enough present for all my birthdays, Luca."

"Maybe."

But even still …

"How about a kiss, then?" she asked, her grin turning almost *demure*. Like she knew exactly what she asked for, but her shyness couldn't help but make an appearance when she pressed her lips together and stared at the floor instead of him. "I never had a real *first kiss*. Could I have one of those for a birthday present? I think that would be sufficient, don't—"

Luca should have said no. A big part of him screamed to do just that, too. If he were a better man, the kind of man he *tried* to be, then he would have refused. He was also her friend even if that meant a lot of things—and shit … she did have the nerve to ask him.

He also didn't want to say no.

Before Penny had even finished what she was saying, Luca stepped in closer to her. His hands found her waist when her head tipped back, so she could stare up at him. Without warning, he dropped his mouth down, lips locking over top of hers for a soft, stroking kiss that despite not going deeper, still managed to set flames alight in his chest. Even his heart raced against the flames.

*Crazy.*

He kissed her once—then twice.

The third time, her lips trembled against his as he started to pull away, and her shaky breath echoed between them. Then, he kissed the tip of her nose. And the top of her head. He didn't let go of her waist, and Penny's hands came to tighten around his wrists like she was trying to keep them right there in that moment. There was something incredibly innocent and enthralling about the way she let her tongue sweep the seam of her lips for a taste of him as she glanced up to meet his gaze again.

"Thank you," she whispered.

Luca only smiled back. "Happy birthday, Penny."

• • •

Luca was perfectly content to sleep until the afternoon after the night of Penny's eighteenth birthday party simply because he could. He didn't have an early morning class, no lecture to race to, *and* all business for the family side of things was on hold while everyone recuperated from their celebration.

Italians knew how to party.

*And* rest.

With no place to go or be, Luca couldn't find a reason to roll his ass out of bed at a decent hour. Shit, this might be the only time he *was* able to sleep in for months. Maybe even years. Who was he to say?

If only everyone else agreed …

It was the sharp ring of his phone—the piercing ringtone he'd chosen for Naz's number snatching Luca from his slumber instantly—that fucked it all up. He could have ignored the call. Even considered it when he saw the digital alarm clock said it wasn't even nine in the goddamn morning.

Except it was Naz.

So …

"Fuck," Luca grumbled, rolling to the side in the bed under the fluffy comforter to reach for the cell phone ringing on the nightstand. He almost dropped the phone as he tried to blink awake and answer the call at the same time. Feeling like more of an idiot, he shoved the phone hard against the side of his face and mumbled, "*What?*"

"She's gone."

That was all Naz said.

*She's gone.*

Luca blinked again and sat up in the bed, scrubbing a hand down his face to wipe away the sleep when he asked, "I don't understand. What—*who?*"

"She's gone, man. Penny. *She's gone.*"

He thought his lack of comprehension and his slowness to catch up was just that he had woken up. Quickly, he understood it was simply because none of this made sense.

"Naz, I talked to Penny last night. *Everybody did.* She was happy. Are you sure she's not just taking a walk or some—"

"She's fucking *gone*—left her shit, took *mine*. Left a note, too."

No way.

"Naz—"

"Remember the program I created? The one that scours the dark web for sexual predators?"

Of course.

Hell, the whole set up Naz made stayed at Luca's place for a while just to keep Roz from stumbling on it. Eventually, his friend moved the system to his own home, satisfied that it wouldn't be bothered or a problem.

Luca hadn't asked about it since.

"She took files I had for it and the mainframe … the laptop," Naz murmured. "Luca, she took everything."

"And she's—"

"Gone," his friend deadpanned. "Yeah."

Now, Luca was out of the bed and entirely awake. He wasn't neat or kind about the way he tore into his closet looking for something suitable to throw on as fast as he could when he asked Naz, "You said she left a note?"

"Yeah, but it's—"

"What did it say?"

"Nothing, really. A thank you. She apologized."

Luca came to a stop in the doorway of the closet, swallowing the lump that lodged in his throat to ask, "Anything else?"

"And she loves us." Naz let out a harsh sound. "How the hell did she even *leave?* She barely even leaves the house! She doesn't have a car or … *where is she?*"

"We'll figure it out."

Or he would.

*Somehow.*

"I'm on my way," Luca told his friend.

He didn't know it then, but what started as a frantic morning would be the beginning of a long, five-year search. He hadn't been ready. In the end, he would sacrifice what had once been his life just to find her.

How could he be ready?

Penny didn't give him a choice.

# *18.*

*Penny*

DESOLATE land surrounded all four points of the vehicle. In the backseat, Penny stared out the window to her left and watched the miles of desert pass them by with every second. She didn't know where they were other than *somewhere* in Nevada. She only knew that because the pilot on the private jet that delivered her to the state had announced their arrival.

Were they still in the state?

She didn't have a clue.

They had certainly been driving long enough to feel like they crossed several states. *Well*, not really, but still …

It was also hard to see anything outside the car, except for the shape of the land, because of the darkness. Not that she figured there would be very much to see even if it *was* daylight. Nothing was still nothing, even in the light of day.

Penny had never done well with long car trips. It was the only time she couldn't seem to sit still and found herself more willing to talk. Maybe that was why she asked the driver, who hadn't even *offered* to speak to her, "How much longer?"

She saw his gaze dart to the rearview mirror, but otherwise, he didn't act like she said anything. Or rather, that he didn't hear her.

Penny wasn't done trying, though. "Where are we?"

A sigh echoed from the front of the car. Maybe that should have been a warning for her to drop it—a sign of the man's irritation with her sudden questions. She just didn't care.

"Are we almost there, or—"

"My job," the man said dryly, even his tone speaking of how bored he was, "is to move you from New York to Nevada. Accompany you. Keep you in one piece while you travel. Make sure you don't … take off."

Penny swallowed hard. "Yeah, so?"

"My job is not to talk to you, entertain you, or answer your questions. Remember?"

*Right.*

She should have expected that.

In fact, she had been told those exact words when a folder had been placed in her hands before she boarded the private jet at a private airstrip in New York. She glanced down at the matte cover of the black folder, her fingers itching to flip open the front and see what waited inside. The warning in the back of her mind stopped her from doing just that.

*Don't open the folder*, Cross had told her. *It's not for you. Think of it … like a test. Your first of many after this, I'm sure. It's not yours. And it's certainly not yours to read. You're going to deliver it.*

To what?

That's what she wanted to know.

The man had only shrugged and said, *To the rest of your life, maybe.*

She hadn't really known what he meant, and maybe a part of her was too scared to ask him to clarify. He said he could help—that he knew people who could make it all go away. There was just one thing …

*We can protect them,* he told her*, but it won't be easy.*

There was a small part of Penny that was aware she wouldn't be ready for what came next. The red flags started in New York when she had to leave the night of her eighteenth birthday party after the house was asleep, and no one would know she was gone until the morning.

By then, it was already too late.

The red flags kept popping up that this wasn't something simple or easily undone when she had been asked to collect the data and devices Naz had been using to crawl the dark web.

*We'll get them all—every last one of them.*

She held onto those words.

Repeated them like a mantra.

As long as this made everyone safe again, then that's all Penny wanted. Or, that's what she kept telling herself when the fear thrummed with every beat of her heart in the backseat. What else could she do?

• • •

The complex of buildings seemed to rise up out of the desert from nowhere. Penny didn't even realize it was there … until it *was.*

She didn't know what to make of the tan, cement walls. From the piece of the building that she could see—along the side where they parked—there weren't any windows despite the section jutting up from the foundation at least three stories high. Their vehicle had parked in front of two black, metal doors that didn't even have handles on the outside.

The camera and security light overtop those doors, however, made it clear the place was active. In some way. The camera blinked with a red light while a streak of bright yellow illuminated a small patch of ground in front of the doors. Likely giving the camera a decent view of anyone who dared to step in view.

The driver put the car in park, and without a word, stepped out of the vehicle. He rounded the back to her door, and opened it up, telling her,

"Step out."

Nope.

"What is this place?" Penny asked.

She didn't move from the backseat.

*Refused.*

Not until she got some kind of answer.

The man simply stared at her, repeating, "Step out."

The look he gave her suggested that the next time he had to tell her to follow one of his orders, he was going to make her do it. Penny really didn't want that to happen, and she didn't want to test his patience when she had probably already done that enough on the drive there. Instead of asking again, she unbuckled the seatbelt and exited the car clutching the black folder tight to her chest.

The wind whipped around them.

It tasted … *dry.*

Definitely still in Nevada.

At least that was something.

Or rather, she *knew* something.

"Here, you'll need this for entrance," the man said, holding out an item for her to take.

Penny eyed the small card stuck between his two fingers before she snatched it from his grasp. Not meeting his gaze, she flipped the thick paper over in her palm to see what it was—or what was on it, for that matter. It was small like a business card, matte black on both sides, but one was different.

A small gold circle encompassed an *L* written in a scripted font. Coiled around the letter was a single snake. The reptile stared out at her from the card with eyes that seemed to lock onto hers without mercy. She'd never been one for snakes, honestly.

"What is this?" she asked.

"Likely your salvation, girl."

*What?*

Penny knew better than to ask.

He wouldn't answer anyway.

"Show it to the camera," he added. "At the doors."

And then, she watched as he got into the car and left. That was it. Penny was alone.

Well, *mostly.*

The building with the black doors still waited for her. Looming at her back, she couldn't possibly forget it was there while she watched tail lights disappear into the darkness.

• • •

The card with the snake did get her inside the building after she held it up high under the light for the camera to clearly see. That was only after she stood in the darkness for more minutes than she cared to admit.

Fear was a terrible thing.

It controlled Penny even when she didn't want it to. That seemed to be her entire life in a goddamn nutshell.

The fear didn't get better when she entered the strange building. Darkness still greeted her. Empty hallways with locked doors guided her through a strange maze of stairwells and passages. No one spoke. Cameras watched her at every angle. It seemed like the place was full of ghosts.

Nothing she could see, but things she could *feel* …

If that made sense.

She simply kept walking. If a door was open, then she went through it. If a hallway led her to a stairwell, then she took it.

Eventually, she came to stand in the doorway of what looked to be an office. Although … certainly not a normal office space. The large glass and metal desk dominated the room. Walls were made up of screens that showcased camera views from every angle. The brightness of the screens contrasted against the shape of two men standing behind the desk.

One was taller than the other. He also had braided his slick, black hair neatly over his shoulder. *He* was the one who smiled at her.

The other man?

He simply stared.

Cold and calculating.

"Hi, I'm—"

"Put the file on the desk," the man on the right said. The one with the icy stare and his silk button-down rolled up to his elbows. "Introductions are not important."

She did what he asked.

Only because he didn't offer an alternative.

Once she stepped away from the desk, the man moved forward and picked up the file. The man with the braid leaned sideways a bit to peek at what was inside the file. It was the way he lifted his brow and nodded, clearly interested in whatever he was reading, that had Penny's heart thumping harder in her chest.

"I don't understand what this place is," she said, wishing *anyone* would talk to her.

All this silence was deafening.

"Or why I had to come here," she added.

The man with the braid gave her a rueful smile. "It appears you're here because your boss wants a weapon. A very specialized weapon. One we can provide."

The other man nodded, snapping the folder closed. "Cree is right."

"Mark that one down," Cree said in a chuckle, "It's not often Dare says *that*. I like to keep count."

Penny was so confused. "What?"

The man named Dare lifted a hand like he was showing her the space—or maybe *everything* surrounding them including the building—when he said, "Welcome to The League, Penny Dunsworth."

# *19.*

*Luca*

"NU-NU lu-lu," the one-year-old babbled.

Leaning in the rear passenger window, Luca tickled the cheek of his nephew. "Uncle Luca, yeah, dude. Nu-nu-lu-lu."

It was the most little Cross could get out. The kid had ma and dad down. He reached for things he wanted and was attempting to at least copy the sounds of some words when it was something that interested him. Luca was working on getting the baby to say his name, now.

When he could, that was.

And had time.

"Almost," Luca praised the boy.

*Nu-nu lu-lu* was the closest they had ever gotten to actually saying *Uncle Luca* so he was going to count that shit as a win.

Cross grinned back at him, showcasing the two front teeth on the top and bottom that had given him hell growing in. He clapped his chubby hands and laughed. Luca couldn't help but laugh back. There was something about babies—or rather, his godson, in particular—that made him fucking stupid.

Still wasn't keen on having his own. But shit, he loved this kid.

A lot could happen in six months.

Luca learned how to change a kid's diaper because he decided to start taking his godson once a week for a night. It let Naz and Roz get out of the house *together* … without a baby in tow. He also dropped out of college officially because he was tired of trying to swim while his head was barely above water. Pride was a tricky fucking thing when a man like him had to admit he failed at something.

He learned that, too.

Six months also saw his sister finally marry his best friend—shit that was probably destined to happen from the moment they met as children but took decades to finally come true. Life was funny like that.

What else happened in six months?

Little Cross turned one the week before—his godson was starting to develop a personality with every babyish smirk and each squealy laugh.

And absolutely *nothing*.

Nothing related to Penny, that was. Because six months was the amount of time Luca had spent looking for even a *scrap* of her existence. It was like piece by piece, she started to disappear. The fact she existed in the first place was slowly erased in every way.

It started with her physical disappearance. The biggest part of the entire puzzle—what started everything. He realized there was nothing on *paper* to say she had actually left or been taken. They did have video, though.

Security camera footage of Naz's place showed Penny taking the external hard drive and other devices attached to his dark web program, writing a note, and leaving. She got into the back of a waiting vehicle that was blacked out on all four corners.

And that was it.

He went into her accounts, first. Bank. Email. Anything to find something. A purchase, even, that would start him out when he realized she left of her own will. He couldn't find a plane, bus or train ticket in her name—*nothing*. Any legal way to track Penny came up with the same, and he exhausted those options fast, but he had already moved onto the *illegal* ways of finding someone in their world, anyway.

It soon became apparent to Luca that even though Penny had left on her own … something wasn't right about it. It was fine if *she* wanted to go and did so. Not fine … but legally, fine.

She was eighteen.

The girl could come and go.

Except why did she start to disappear everywhere else, too? Records of Penny Dunsworth started to vanish one by one. Every time Luca went looking for something from her past that might help to lead him to her … he found less and less.

Digital yearbooks gone.

School records suddenly … missing.

Hospital data, deleted.

Shit that shouldn't happen.

That usually *didn't* happen.

Someone was making any trace of Penny just … disappear, he quickly realized. Like she did to them.

And then one after another, Luca's days became consumed with finding her. Or even anything at all about her. The next thing that might vanish after he found it … or just before he did, for that matter. It was only now that he had finally decided to start contacting organizations across North America to find the ghost he was chasing.

Hopefully, that would lead him somewhere new.

Somewhere toward Penny.

Or *anything*.

Then, maybe he could tell his friend—

"Nu-nu lu-lu," Cross shouted inside the car, the sudden loudness making Luca blink out of his thoughts violently as the boy grabbed the stuffed bear with the blue bow from his lap. He gave the paw a squeeze the way they had been doing for him for months, and an all too familiar song started to play. "Yay!"

Luca smiled or tried. "Yeah, yay, buddy."

Baby duty was something.

He tried to help when he could, though. Like when Naz had to report to tribute for Cosa Nostra and didn't have someone to keep an eye on the baby when it was supposed to be his day to look after the little guy. That was why Luca currently entertained baby Cross while his father did business with the rest of the family's men in a diner across the street.

Luca wasn't made.

And as his focus drifted away from not only college but *famiglia* business as well, while he searched for Penny … some people made it all too clear that he wasn't welcomed now. Made or not. Some men in the family said nothing, and others said too much.

Soon, the diner started to clear out. Luca wasn't surprised to see Naz vacate the restaurant last as he had probably stayed behind to speak to his father, and Zeke. Shit, his best friend was talking to his own father more than even he was lately.

It couldn't be helped.

It was probably better this way.

Naz made a beeline for Luca, but greeted his son before saying anything to his friend. "Hey, little man. See, Daddy told you I'd be right back." Then, to Luca, he added, "Thanks for keeping an eye on him. Tribute was supposed to be tomo—"

"It's cool, man. No worries."

Naz must have heard Luca's distant tone because he straightened up and turned to look at what had caught his friend's attention across the street. Cross had come to stand on the sidewalk outside the restaurant with Luca's father at his side.

Zeke stared his way.

Luca watched back.

His father was one of those unhappy men—the disappointment was no longer loudly voiced, simply felt and understood between the two of them.

"Did you find anything this week?" Naz asked.

About Penny, he meant.

Luca didn't need clarification.

*Everything* was about Penny lately.

"Nothing. What if she doesn't want to be found? None of this makes any sense, Naz."

"*Something* happened. And I want answers. Roz barely sleeps. I wake up, and she's crying about her. I promised her … I have to at least try."

"You mean *me*."

Naz gave him a look.

Luca only shrugged. "Yeah, I know."

Naz would if he could, but as he'd been told over and over the past few months … *famiglia* first. The mafia always got its way.

No matter what.

"I'll find her, Naz. It's just … *when*."

And how.

# *CODA.*

*Present Day …*

"*CROSS*! Get back to the house, son! Time to eat!"

Penny's head snapped to the side, gaze darting over her shoulder through the trees to find the form of a man coming to stand on the rear porch of the three-level home. Like his son, she hadn't laid eyes on Nazio in as many years.

Not much had changed.

He was older, yes, but his playful grin as he called for his child still felt like a welcomed sight to her.

"Cross!" he called again.

The little boy just a few feet away looked her way with a shrug. "You're gonna leave now, huh?"

"I have to."

He nodded once. "Yeah, you keep doing that to people, I guess. *Leaving*."

Penny blinked away the veil of tears that shrouded her vision. "I don't want to, though."

"*Cross Nazio Donati*—time to eat, kiddo!"

As if on cue, Cross's stomach growled. He didn't even look sheepish about it.

"The interlude—the part of the song that repeats, right?" he asked her.

She smiled. "Yeah, what about it?"

"Mine feels like a hug."

Penny stilled.

He couldn't know that …

It wasn't possible.

"It does," he said again. "It feels like a hug when I hear it. I feel the same. Light at first. But then it tightens, *muffles*. Like arms wrapping around me, bringing me closer, getting warmer and tighter."

"I composed a lullaby for you. That's all."

Cross kicked at the dirt when his father called his name again. "Yeah, but with a hug. Right?"

"The way I thought a hug should feel. If someone made one with music. If I could hug you through mine."

Not that she ever told anyone that fact.

"Okay." Cross turned back toward the house. "That's what I thought."

"Cross, are you in those damn woods again?"

Penny sucked in a sharp breath at the sight of Nazio strolling down the steps of the porch and heading their way. Toward the woods.

"I have to—"

Penny didn't even get to finish her sentence before the boy had turned back around. He darted for her, his small arms wrapping around her middle. The hug was light at first, and then it tightened with warmth.

"Please don't tell them you saw me," she whispered, hugging the boy back. "I only want to help them, okay?"

If she could have stayed right there in that moment with a piece of her past cementing her between *then* and *now*, she would have. Forever.

"I won't tell." Cross peered up at her when he took a step back and let her go, asking, "You'll come back, won't you?"

She chose not to lie.

"I'm sure gonna try."

• • •

Want to continue Penny and Luca's story – grab *ONE SECOND AFTER ANOTHER* by visiting bethanykris.com/OneSecond!

# *ABOUT THE AUTHOR*

Bethany-Kris is a Canadian author, lover of much, and mother to four sons, three cats, and four dogs. A small town in Eastern Canada where she was born and raised is where she has always called home. With her boys under her feet, a snuggling cat, barking dogs, and a spouse calling over his shoulder, she is nearly always writing something ... when she can find the time.

Find Bethany-Kris at her:

www.bethanykris.com

# *OTHER BOOKS*

The After Another Trilogy

One Step After Another
One Breath After Another
One Second After Another

Boykov Bratva

Fractured Ties
Essence of Fear

The Guzzi Legacy

Corrado
Alessio
Chris
Beni
Bene
Marcus

Renzo + Lucia

Privilege
Harbor
Contempt
Forever
Cusp
Renzo + Lucia: The Complete Trilogy

Andino + Haven

Duty
Vow
One Last Time
Andino + Haven: The Complete Duet

John + Siena

Loyalty
Disgrace
John + Siena: The Complete Duet
John + Siena: Extended

Cross + Catherine

Always
Revere
Unruly
The Companion
Naz & Roz

Guzzi Duet

Unraveled, Book One
Entangled, Book Two
Cara & Gian: The Complete Duet

DeLuca Duet

Waste of Worth: Part One
Worth of Waste: Part Two

Filthy Marcellos

Antony
Lucian
Giovanni
Dante
Legacy
A Very Marcello Christmas
The Complete Collection

Donati Bloodlines

Thin Lies
Thin Lines
Thin Lives
Behind the Bloodlines
The Complete Trilogy

Standalone Titles

Pink
Pretty Lies
Dirty Pool
Effortless
Inflict
Cozen
Captivated
Dishonored

Seasons of Betrayal

Where the Sun Hides
Where the Snow Falls
Where the Wind Whispers
Seasons: The Complete Seasons of Betrayal Series

Gun Moll Trilogy

Gun Moll
Gangster Moll
Madame Moll

The Chicago War

Deathless & Divided
Reckless & Ruined
Scarless & Sacred
Breathless & Bloodstained
The Complete Series
Maldives & Mistletoe

The Russian Guns

The Arrangement
The Life
The Score
Demyan & Ana
Shattered
The Jersey Vignettes

FANTASY ROMANCE

The Hunted: A 9INE REALMS Novel

Find more on Bethany-Kris's website at www.bethanykris.com.

www.ingramcontent.com/pod-product-compliance
Lightning Source LLC
LaVergne TN
LVHW010704110826
845149LV00014B/3227

* 9 7 8 1 9 8 9 6 5 8 3 2 1 *